W9-AWP-693

"What do you intend to do with me?"

Julia's voice was a whisper, cold with fear.

"You? Well, I've had several plans in the last twenty-four hours.

Originally, I had intended to trade Señor Lennox to the president in return for certain concessions."

"Why can't you trade Señorita Lennox then?" Julia asked as calmly as she could.

"I thought it unchivalrous," Madariago said, laughing harshly. "But you have convinced me that I must be less sexist."

"And if the president doesn't agree to your concessions?"

Madariago was leaving, but he turned to look her over coolly. "Then I can think of a way you might make yourself useful."

Useful. It had a workaday sound, like housework or typing letters. She frowned. "Useful to your operation?"

The smile grew. "Useful to me," he corrected gently. And the smile was gone.

SOPHIE WESTON wrote and illustrated her first book—at the age of five. After university she decided on a career in international finance, which was tremendously stimulating and demanding, but it was not enough. Something was missing in her life, and that something turned out to be writing. These days her life is complete. She loves exciting travel and adventure yet hates to stray too long from her homey cottage in Chelsea, where she writes.

Books by Sophie Weston

HARLEQUIN PRESENTS
838—EXECUTIVE LADY
870—A STRANGER'S TOUCH
918—LIKE ENEMIES
942—SHADOW PRINCESS
957—YESTERDAY'S MIRROR

HARLEQUIN ROMANCE
1925—BEWARE THE HUNTSMAN
2005—GOBLIN COURT
2129—WIFE TO CHARLES
2218—UNEXPECTED HAZARD
2362—AN UNDEFENDED CITY

Don't miss any of our special offers. Write to us at the following address for information on our newest releases.

Harlequin Reader Service
901 Fuhrmann Blvd., P.O. Box 1397, Buffalo, NY 14240
Canadian address: P.O. Box 603,
Fort Erie, Ont. L2A 5X3

SOPHIE WESTON

beyond ransom

Harlequin Books

TORONTO • NEW YORK • LONDON
AMSTERDAM • PARIS • SYDNEY • HAMBURG
STOCKHOLM • ATHENS • TOKYO • MILAN

Harlequin Presents first edition May 1987
ISBN 0-373-10980-6

Original hardcover edition published in 1986
by Mills & Boon Limited

Copyright © 1986 by Sophie Weston. All rights reserved.
Philippine copyright 1986. Australian copyright 1986.
Cover illustration copyright © 1987 by Tony Meers.
Except for use in any review, the reproduction or utilization of
this work in whole or in part in any form by any electronic,
mechanical or other means, now known or hereafter invented,
including xerography, photocopying and recording, or in any
information storage or retrieval system, is forbidden without
the permission of the publisher, Harlequin Enterprises Limited,
225 Duncan Mill Road, Don Mills, Ontario, Canada M3B 3K9.

All the characters in this book have no existence outside the
imagination of the author and have no relation whatsoever to
anyone bearing the same name or names. They are not even
distantly inspired by any individual known or unknown to the
author, and all incidents are pure invention.

The Harlequin trademarks, consisting of the words
HARLEQUIN PRESENTS and the portrayal of a Harlequin,
are trademarks of Harlequin Enterprises Limited and are
registered in the Canada Trade Marks Office; the portrayal
of a Harlequin is registered in the United States Patent
and Trademarks Office.

Printed in U.S.A.

CHAPTER ONE

THE music in the nightclub grew louder after the floor show, thought Julia Lennox, wincing. She would not have believed it possible. She looked at her watch surreptitiously. Not yet midnight!

Seeing the movement Larry Davidson leaned across to her, unnoticed by their guests who were exchanging *badinage* with two of the professional hostesses employed by the club.

'Have you had enough?' Larry asked under his breath.

For a moment Julia was tempted. She had had a hard day. She had negotiated hard all morning, bringing every ounce of her considerable professional skill to the talks, and now she was almost certain it had been for nothing. She was feeling tired, she had a raging headache, and the raucous jollity of the city's most expensive nightclub was having a depressing effect on her spirits.

But it was part of her job and, until the President actually told her that Technica Associates had not got the contract, she was in charge. She managed a wan smile at Larry.

'No, I'll stick it out,' she said. 'It's quite an experience.'

He shrugged. 'If you say so.'

Larry was looking bored. Unlike Julia, to whom he had been assigned as assistant on this mission, he was an old Central American hand. His Spanish was fluent, though even Julia could detect the Milwaukee accent. And it was Larry who had discovered that this was the place Finance Ministry officials expected to be entertained by visiting businessmen with projects to sell.

I should be grateful to him, thought Julia, shifting on

her velvet covered chair. At least our guests seem to be enjoying themselves.

They had thrown themselves into an orgy of rich food and imported whisky. The drinks were brought by beautiful girls, with wide practised smiles and evening dresses cut away in every conceivable place. The Ministry officials had been embarrassed at first, unnaturally restrained in Julia's presence. But under the influence of Scotch and Julia's imperturbability, they had relaxed. By now they were chatting up the girls as cheerfully as if their host for the evening really was, as they would clearly have preferred, the man they had expected.

Larry too thought she would cast a damper on the evening. He had made no secret of it. But Julia had said firmly that if she was authorising a substantial amount of entertaining expenditure, she was honour bound to play host herself. Larry had muttered that she would not enjoy herself and, she thought wryly, he was not wrong. On the other hand she was not embarrassed by the blatant sexiness of the girls. Beneath their fixed smiles one or two of them looked as tired as Julia. She felt a certain fellow feeling for them. Any minute now she, too, would have to dance with one of her slightly drunken guests.

It was as she was walking on to the dance floor with the senior Ministry official that she felt herself being watched. She had a sharp prickling sensation in the back of the neck and her head turned almost involuntarily to see who it was who was causing her discomfort.

He was standing in the doorway, just in front of the tasselled velvet curtain which masked the exit. He was in a dinner jacket, as were most of the men in the club, and had obviously just handed to a bowing attendant some sort of coat and a long white scarf. He was in the act of stripping off his gloves but he seemed to have stilled in mid-action while he inspected her through narrowed eyes.

Startled, Julia stopped dead. He was looking her over very thoroughly, from head to toe, his gaze dismissive and faintly contemptuous and yet—something else, what was it? She suddenly realised where she had seen the expression before. Her professor at university had looked in exactly that way down a telescope at some fascinating but disgusting insect. That was how the man looked; fascinated in spite of himself.

Forgetful of her surroundings, she stared back at him. He was tall, taller by head and shoulders than his three companions, and lithe as a runner, but it was his face that was unforgettable. In the uncertain light Julia could not make out whether he was dark or fair, but she could see all too clearly the high cheekbones, the slightly slanted eyes set under brows steeply marked enough to give him the look of the devil. It was not a reassuring face. She gave a little shiver.

Her companion noticed and followed her gaze.

'Ah, Don Roberto is here,' he said in an odd voice. 'You know him, *señorita*?'

'No,' Julia said slowly, wondering if it was true. She could not remember him, yet he was looking at her so intently it seemed as if she ought to do so. But surely this was not the sort of man she could have let slip out of her memory?

'Señor Roberto Madariaga. He is a lawyer—a very rich and successful lawyer. He does much work for the international companies. You are sure you do not know him?'

Julia shook her head. 'I've never even heard the name.'

'No?' It seemed to her that her companion relaxed. 'Ah well, there are other lawyers, after all, and Don Roberto has—' he hesitated '—widened his interests these days. Or so they tell me.'

He touched her arm and steered her gently on to the dance floor. Julia could no longer see the new arrival. Breaking that contact felt like cutting a bond, an almost physical shock. She shook her head, slightly bewildered by the effect his idle glance had had on her.

It must be the overpowering noise, she told herself. Or the dim lighting. Both had a distorting, disorientating effect. Otherwise she would not have noticed his scrutiny or allowed herself to be upset by it. It was not like her at all.

Her companion was doing his best to make polite conversation with her.

'This is your first visit to Alto Rio, *señorita*?'

'Yes,' she agreed.

'I hope while you have been here you have been able to see something of my country.'

'Very little, I'm afraid. Larry and I have not really had time for tourism.'

'Alas, we have very little tourism in Oaxacan. For us it is still a new industry. And we have the problem of the mountains: so many foreigners who come here are ill at first because of the altitude.'

'So I've been told. I must be very lucky—I've felt fine,' Julia said.

The Ministry official looked amused. 'Ah, here in Alto Rio we are not *high, señorita*. A matter of nine thousand feet only. It is the hinterland which is high—there are villages at fifteen and sixteen thousand feet. Of course, they are the interesting ones, where there are the old crafts and the pre-conquest ruins.' He shrugged. 'And they are the ones where it makes the tourists sick to visit. It is most annoying.'

'It must be.' Julia was answering him at random. The smooth movements of the dance had brought her round to face the entrance again and the man was still there, still watching her.

The waiter had gone now and so had his companions, presumably following the attendant to their table. So he was left alone, staring out across the heads of the unconscious diners, his eyes fixed on Julia with an oddly speculative expression. She did not like that expression. She put up her chin.

Suddenly his eyes lifted, became aware. He almost jumped, as if he had come to himself somewhere quite foreign to him. Their eyes met and locked, and Julia felt a fierce sensation, almost like pain, shoot through her spine. Her eyes widened.

Don Roberto seemed as disconcerted by that lightning contact as she, but he recovered himself faster. While she was still dancing, swaying mechanically to the strident music, he had already half turned to follow his friends. But in doing so he did not take his eyes off her. Rather, the half smile with which he had been studying her grew. He had a long, mobile mouth which looked as if he might be very passionate or very cruel or very demanding, not least of himself. Julia gave a little shiver. She was very nearly certain that he sensed it, though it was so slight that it missed the man in whose arms she was dancing.

She swallowed, suddenly and inexplicably alarmed. And because she was not used to being alarmed by chance contacts and did not like the sensation, bravado induced her to give him a deliberate smile. It was a dare, and she knew it. It dared him to pretend that he had not been watching her, not been following her round the room with his eyes.

If Julia hoped to disconcert him she was disappointed. He looked surprised for an instant, those elegant eyebrows rising. Then the surprise was replaced by amusement. He half turned towards the dance floor and made her an elaborataly courteous bow.

Julia blushed, instantly and comprehensively. He smiled at her, almost intimately, as if they knew each other and knew a good deal more than simple friends would do, then turned his shoulder and strolled unhurriedly to join his friends.

The Ministry official had not missed that little

interchange, even though he had not noticed so much else.

'It seems that Don Roberto knows you, *señorita*,' he said in a voice which sounded troubled. 'Or at least hopes to do so.'

Julia took hold of herself with an effort. 'Nonsense! I expect he mistook me for someone else. It's so dimly lit in here, it must be very easy to do.' And she returned firmly to the discarded subject of Indian crafts and Oaxacate-can ruins.

At their table Larry was discussing American football with the other guest, who was making little attempt to disguise his boredom. Over Larry's shoulder he was ogling a pretty girl in what appeared to be a gold lamé swimsuit who was selling cigarettes and cheroots. Larry, who did not smoke, had observed neither the girl nor the fact that his companion's attention had wandered.

Julia was seating herself when her companion said abruptly in his thick, locally accented Spanish, 'Madariaga is here. Looking for someone, I'd say.'

The other looked distinctly alarmed. 'Who? Not us?'

Julia lowered her eyes to hide the sudden keenness in them. She had judged it best to disguise the fluency of her Spanish, letting Larry do most of the talking in that language. It suited their customers better and it meant that they were not so guarded in her presence when they thought she could only half understand what they were saying to each other.

Larry became aware of their low-voiced conversation. 'Have you seen someone you know?'

The older one, the one with whom Julia had been dancing, recovered himself faster. 'Oh, in Alto Rio it is impossible not to. It is not like New York, you know. Here you see people you know on every street corner. Over there, for instance . . .'

And he began to point out the local celebrities who were patronising the club tonight.

Larry and Julia listened with interest and Julia stored many of the names away for future reference. After all, even if this expedition failed, that was not to say that she would not return here in the future with new projects, other packages. It could be useful to know who were the right people to approach when that time came.

But all the same, she had the impression that her companions were talking at random, almost as if they were trying to distract her from the subject that had originally started the subject. Madariaga's name was not mentioned.

Yet he was still in the club; one swift glance told Julia exactly where he was sitting and with whom. He was at a table under a graceful palm, on the raised dais that projected round the stage and the little orchestra. He was with two other men and a spectacularly beautiful woman. She was dressed in glimmering satin, printed with bold geometric patterns that looked as if, like the lady, it had come straight from Paris. She looked very bored.

Only one of the party was talking, and he was talking a lot, nodding his head to emphasise his points, and waving his hands. Madariaga watched impassively. He sat in profile to Julia. It was an arrogant profile and his expression was not encouraging. She thought that if she had been the man who was talking she would have been intimidated into silence now. The third man was smoking nervously, lighting one cigarillo from another and then grinding it out only half-smoked. He spoke briefly from time to time and was ignored. His eyes moved restlessly all the time between the man who was speaking and Madariaga.

The lighting dimmed suddenly. The disco record finished and the disc jockey left his seat to desultory applause. The tiny band had returned and broke into a cool samba. They were surprisingly good.

'Ah!' Beside her, the men from the Ministry sat up in

clear expectation. The younger one said under his breath, '*That* is why Madariaga is here!'

'Florita?' The other sounded unconvinced. 'You may be right, but . . .'

They were hushed by the waiters and their fellow diners. A green spotlight had been thrown on to the small stage and some rather rickety-looking scenery was being manoeuvred into place. There was a distinct rustle of expectancy in the audience.

'What's happening?' asked Julia.

The older man answered her. 'Florita is to dance. She is very famous. She travels internationally. She sometimes dances here when she is home, but—' he shrugged, 'she is not often home and she is very temperamental. So they don't dare to advertise it in advance in case she doesn't turn up.' His voice became cynical. 'It is a rare privilege to see Florita dance. If Señor Madariaga were not here tonight, I doubt whether you would do so.'

And then he fell silent, for there was a faint percussive pause in the music and then, to a storm of applause, the dancer walked on to the stage.

Julia's first thought was that Florita was very beautiful: she was slim and tanned with a mane of tawny lion's hair and flashing brown eyes. The second was, that for all the girl's professional grace and undoubted sensuality, she looked worried, almost preoccupied. She did not falter in her dancing, though, which was fast and athletic and was rapturously received.

Larry leaned forward. 'Isn't she *gorgeous*?' he exclaimed, revealing that beneath the manner of the international businessman there was still the boy not long out of college.

'Beautiful,' agreed Julia, as the dancer bowed and prepared to go into her next routine.

Julia thought the girl had cast an anxious look up in the direction of Madariaga's table, but she could not be sure. There was something that disturbed her about that look,

almost the whole scene, but she could not put her finger
on it. It felt somehow as if Roberto Madariaga, for all his
patrician air of detachment, was part of a performance
that was being staged for the benefit of some very
specific object. And Julia felt in her bones that that
object boded no good to herself or Larry.

She tried to rid herself of the feeling as Florita danced,
winding her way sinuously through the tables. It was
silly, she told herself. Even if there was some plot afoot, it
could have nothing to do with her. Perhaps they were
going to run away together, thereby breaking her
contract and his marriage. Perhaps they were about to
ruin both their careers for their mutual passion. Yes, that
was better. High melodrama, certainly, but nothing to do
with Julia Lennox of Technica Associates who had seen
the President this afternoon, lost the contract she was
supposed to finalise, and would be returning on the first
plane to New York tomorrow.

Florita had been dancing apparently at random but
with a clear underlying direction, Julia noted. Now she
was almost at Madariaga's table, the following spotlight
catching him intermittently on its edge. He was
frowning.

Then, unexpectedly, Florita began to dance round one
of the cigarette waitresses. The girl laughed, the audience
laughed and so too did Florita, though Julia thought she
looked too intent to be carefree. But perhaps she was just
concentrating on her dancing. She was certainly marvel-
lously accomplished.

Florita whipped one of the fat cigars out of the girl's
tray, waving it alluringly under the noses of the nearby
diners who pantomimed appreciation. She removed the
ring label and began to cut the end of the cigar, making
incisions with her long, gold-painted nails. The band had
tuned down to a whisper above the rustling rhythms of
brush on drum.

Into the spotlight came a hand with a flaming lighter.

Florita bent, lit the cigar, and inhaled luxuriously several
times. The hand was withdrawn but she was already
turning towards it. The spotlight was full on the table as
Florita danced alluringly towards Roberto Madariaga
and held out the cigar towards him. For a long moment
they looked at each other and Julia had the feeling that a
message had passed between them, though she could not
see that either of them spoke. Then he reached out a hand
and allowed her to give him the cigar. Smoke wafted up
from it, grey in the spotlight. He put it to his lips and,
deliberately, blew a cloud of smoke straight at the girl.

Florita did not seem in the least offended. She put her
hands together and bowed in a little Eastern gesture of
submission and danced backwards, her tawny head bent.
Julia was fairly certain she was mocking him, though she
could not have said why. The tune rose again, as Florita
made her rounds of the balcony, taking here a puff of a
gentleman's cigarette, here a sip of another one's wine,
and always moving on before they could touch her.

And then, suddenly, Julia realised that she was
making her way to their table. She stiffened instinctively.
Why, oh, why did she have this sensation of impending
disaster whenever she looked at Florita? She had learned
to trust her instincts and they were all screaming at her to
get up and leave this nightclub before the girl could speak
to them. Yet it was clearly impossible. The three men
were totally absorbed. So she tried to relax, to smile and
look as if she were enjoying herself.

Florita clearly intended to do the cigar trick again.
Perhaps she did it once on the balcony and once in the
main well of the nightclub, Julia thought, trying to be
sensible and ignore her fears. The dancer stepped lightly
on to the banquette where Larry was sitting and thence to
the table itself. Stepping as delicately as a cat, she did a
neat little step dance among the bottles and glasses, not
overturning one of them. There was a scatter of applause.

Suddenly she stopped, one toe pointed, the multi-

coloured streamers that made up her skirt falling away
from her tanned thigh. She looked down at Larry
unsmilingly. This time she did not make a great
performance about preparing the cigar; she simply held
it out to him and as he half-rose to take it, snatched it
back and rolled it slowly up the length of her exposed
thigh. As it reached the top there was a little explosion,
like the cap of a toy gun, and a rather larger flash, and the
lights all went out.

There was surprised laughter from the audience, a
number of cheers and a surge of applause. Julia,
however, held her breath, half expecting Larry to have
been spirited away in the moment of darkness.

But when the lights came up, he was still there, smiling
faintly sheepishly, with Florita, surprisingly small when
no longer under the spotlight, sitting composedly beside
him on his banquette. She stood up to take several bows
but then seated herself firmly again while the band
swung into dance music.

She turned to Larry with a faintly apologetic grin. 'I
hope you don't mind.' The voice was light and pleasing
and very Manhattan. She did not look so exotic out of the
spotlight either. 'It was a new trick for me and I had to try
it out on somebody who wouldn't grab.'

Julia's eyes narrowed. 'You haven't done the explod-
ing cigar routine before?'

Florita shook her head. 'No. The whole Carmen
extravaganza is new.' She sounded faintly scornful.

'Don't you enjoy it?' asked Larry.

She shrugged. 'What's to enjoy? It's hellish timing and
one drunken bum could louse up the whole thing. They
can keep it. I'm a dancer, not a bloody illusionist.' She
stood up and gave him a speculative glance. 'Hang
around and I'll be back and show you what kind of a
dancer I am—when I have a partner.'

She was gone, flitting among the tables without
stopping though people called out congratulations to her

from all sides. The two Ministry men were looking frankly envious.

'Now *that's* an invitation not to refuse,' the younger one said wistfully. 'I've never heard of her dancing with the customers before.'

'Perhaps she has had an argument with Madariaga and this is her way of punishing him,' said his senior, more cynically.

But Madariaga, at his elevated table, continued to smoke his cigar and appeared unmoved. He had given their table just one, fleeting look, before Florita left them. Since then he had ignored them. Julia tried to comfort herself that at least it did not look as if Larry was going to find himself facing the rage of a jealous lover. But she remained uncomforted and almost jumped out of her skin when their conversation was interrupted by a smooth voice.

'*Señorita*' She turned. It was Madariaga, very cool and handsome and self-possessed, holding out an imperative hand to her. 'Do you care to dance?' He gave Larry an amused look. 'With your permission, of course, *señor*?'

Before Julia could follow all her instincts and refuse, Larry was nodding graciously. She stiffened angrily, but Larry, true to form, remained unaware of it. She was not particularly feminist, but the calm assumption of masculine possession that Madariaga implied and Larry accepted, roused her to fury. For a white-hot second she contemplated telling him that she did not dance and would be glad if he would not annoy her.

But then she remembered—she was selling, and these were the customers and their society and habits were different. She was the foreigner and must respond civilly to what she found. So she stood up with a murmured acquiescence and gave Madariaga her hand. She would, she promised herself, give Larry a lecture on the sort of support that she expected from him all the way from Alto Rio to Miami tomorrow. But tonight she would smile sweetly and bow to the inevitable.

The dance was softly rhythmic but not dreamy. He held her very correctly, not hard, so that their bodies touched lightly, fleetingly as they danced. It was all perfectly ordinary except that Julia had never felt so aware of a man in her life. So aware or so frightened.

To mask it she said coolly, 'Is it your habit to ask strange ladies to dance, Señor Madariaga?'

If she had hoped to disconcert him by knowing his name, she was disappointed. He would no doubt have expected her to enquire, Julia thought, annoyed.

He said, 'Only when they intrigue me, *señorita.*'

He was laughing at her openly. She knew perfectly well that the slight hesitation before the word 'intrigue' was intended to imply that he found her attractive. He would expect her to be flattered by that, she thought in a rage, just as Larry was flattered by the obvious tactics of Florita. She bit her lip.

'Have I offended you?' His voice was soft, husky and, in the right circumstances, no doubt very seductive. Julia could not understand why he should bother to waste this slick approach on herself and once again felt a tremor of inexplicable apprehension. She shivered, in spite of herself.

He noticed. His arms tightened slightly and then relaxed.

'*Have* I offended you?' He sounded surprised and slightly less amused, Julia thought with some satisfaction.

She tipped her head back to look at him. 'Not yet,' she told him in a cool voice.

His brows rose. 'Not yet? You are expecting me to?'

She smiled straight into his eyes. 'I think it very probable,' she said sweetly.

He was taken aback, no question of it.

'But why? Because I ask you to dance?'

'Because you asked my escort whether you could dance

with me,' Julia corrected him.

He shrugged. 'You may not believe this but in my country it would have been very insulting to your escort if I had done anything else. It is a question of courtesy, merely.' He looked sardonic. 'But of course courtesy is considered to be unacceptably sexist in your country, is it not, *señorita*? And is this all your reason for being offended at me?'

'No,' Julia said quietly. 'I don't like men who blow smoke in dancers' faces either.'

There was a pause, then he said slowly, 'You think I was rude to Florita?'

'Señor Madariaga, it is none of my business how you behave to other people. Except,' she added, 'in so far as it is an indication of how you may behave to myself.'

His eyes glinted down at her. They were not the dark brown she had expected but something closer to hazel and as cold as winter rain, even when he appeared, as now, amused.

'You would not like me to treat you as I treat Florita?' he asked in a voice of unholy mockery.

Julia felt a blush rise and was angry at herself. She ought to have more self-possession than that. She ought not to be thrown off balance by the blatant teasing of a practised seducer which was what this man clearly was. She glared at him.

'To be perfectly frank, Señor Madariaga, I would prefer you not to treat me at all,' she said briskly.

He gave a soft laugh. 'But you ask the impossible, *señorita*,' he said in honeyed voice, 'when you are so beautiful that no man worthy of the name could resist you.'

She stared at him, speechless. The flattery was so outrageous that it was funny. Against her will her lips twitched. He met her eyes limpidly; he even managed an ardent sigh. Julia gave up the struggle and laughed aloud, throwing her head back in amusement.

This time his arms tightened about her and did not relax. Inexorably she was drawn closer to him so that she could no longer fail to be aware of the strength of muscle beneath the anonymous suiting.

'Why do you laugh?' He sounded reproachful, but there was that hint of amusement still there as an undercurrent. 'Do you think I am the sort of man who can look on beauty and remain unmoved?'

'Nope.' Julia shook her head and said in a deflating tone, 'I think you're the sort of man who can't resist the chance of encouraging people to make fools of themselves.'

'*Señorita*, you are unkind,' he mourned. 'Do you think I flatter you?'

'I think you're sending me up sky-high,' she informed him roundly.

He sighed again, but there was a gleam in his eye that Julia found distinctly at odds with his romantic demeanour.

'Then it can only be that you do not know how beautiful you are.' He raised her right hand which he was clasping loosely in his to his lips and touched half a dozen little kisses across the back of it, watching her all the time.

She sighed with ostentatious patience. 'Señor Madariaga, I know to the millimetre.'

'I do not believe it.' He shook his head. 'You talk so sharply of millimetres and of being made a fool of. It is all wrong. When you look like a princess out of a man's dreams and feel,' his free hand was moving gently, rhythmically up and down her spine, 'as if he has woken up with his dream in his arms.'

Julia pushed herself a little away from him, bracing herself with her free hand against his chest. She gave him a straight look.

'I find this all a touch overwhelming,' she told him in a neutral voice. 'I don't think I'm suited to heavy compliments after two minutes' acquaintance. They give me the creeps.'

They danced for a few seconds in silence. Then he said, with more than a touch of annoyance in his voice, 'I could wish that you were not so intelligent, *señorita*. Let me tell you, it is very offputting to gaze into misty blue eyes and find yourself being weighed in the balance.'

Julia hid a smile. 'I'm sorry,' she said politely. 'I guess we're just incompatible.' She pulled even further away from him and looked pointedly towards her table. 'So perhaps if we rejoined my escort . . .?'

His brows came together in a quick frown. But he was laughing when he said in that low, husky voice, 'You cannot possibly tell whether or not we are incompatible on the evidence of one dance, little one. And I—who, I imagine, have greater experience in these matters than you—believe we might find that we were very compatible indeed.'

Julia did not answer for a moment. She was shaken, she admitted it to herself. She was pretty sure that the eloquent Señor Madariaga was playing some obscure game with her. She had not yet lost her head, but there was something there, some undeniable spark of attraction, and if she continued to bandy words with him she was very much afraid she might.

He said softly, 'You look so remote, yet so desirable; the unattainable lady in her tower.'

Startled, her eyes met his, wide and questioning. The firm mouth moved in a wry smile.

'I think you do not begin to understand your own power.'

She swallowed, thoroughly disturbed, and spoke brutally to break the mood, the spell that his voice was spinning.

'Señor Madariaga, are you making a pass at me?' she asked lightly.

He was so surprised that he almost stopped dancing.

She felt him falter and then get back into step at once.

Then he said calmly, 'No, *señorita*.' He was laughing down at her, not in the least offended, as far as she could see, nor disconcerted either. 'I hope that, if I wanted to *make love* to you,' the words were emphasised pointedly as a correction to her own harsher phrase, 'you would understand the fact. In spite of my poor English.'

His English was perfect, as he very well knew, fluent and without accent. Julia refused to be humbled.

'So do I,' she said with a sparkle in her eye.

He looked down at her, a smile deep in the cold eyes. 'You will. I promise,' he said softly. And sounded as if he meant it.

CHAPTER TWO

HE was returning her to her table when the lights went out. Without warning, the club was plunged into darkness. Somewhere a woman screamed, and Julia felt his hand under her elbow tighten.

'Do not be concerned.' The husky voice was calm. 'It is simply a power cut—we have many of them in Alto Rio. They are supposed to be scheduled so that people are prepared, but sometimes,' there was a smile in his voice, 'the machinery has a mind of its own. So the management will have plenty of alternative lighting. And here it comes.'

Julia saw that waiters were hurrying from behind the service doors with trays of lighted candles. They went surefootedly round the room, placing a branch on each table. The diners accepted it placidly as if they were used to such scenes.

'Very efficient,' commented Julia, resuming her steps.

Beside her, Madariaga was shaken by a silent laugh. She turned her head to look at him enquiringly.

'Efficient,' he murmured. 'How sadly typical! You do not find flickering candlelight romantic, you find it efficient.'

Julia knew when she was being teased. She sighed. 'You are a romantic, *señor*?'

They were almost at the table. He appeared to consider her question seriously.

'No, I would not normally have described myself as a romantic,' he mused before adding wickedly, 'Though in comparison with you, I probably am.'

'I'm sure you are,' said Julia seating herself composedly and giving him a friendly dismissive smile. 'Thank you
for the dance.'

'The pleasure, *señorita*, was mine,' he assured her
solemnly. 'And I shall hope for it again later—when they
have restored the electricity and the band.' He nodded to
them all impartially and strolled off to his own party.

Under cover of pouring more wine for her, Larry
leaned closer.

'I don't know who he is, but the boys don't like him.'

Julia smiled, sipping her wine, not looking at him, the
soul of discretion as the years had taught her. Larry
moved, turning on his banquette as if to look round the
room, but he carried on murmuring in that low voice.

'They started talking about telling the Minister, maybe
even calling him tonight. I think Madariaga frightens
them. And they sure as hell don't think he was dancing
with you because he fancies you.'

Julia assimilated this information. She had not
thought so either, but it was interesting that his
attentions had so alarmed their guests. So who was he,
apart from being a lawyer? She frowned slightly. Maybe
he was one of that international fraternity that had
contacts in the media all round the world. Maybe he
thought she had a story to tell.

She bit her lip. Well, of course she had, but she would
not. Not if Technica Associates was going to do business
in Central America ever again. Not if she wanted to keep
her reputation for straight dealing. Not if she wanted to
hang on to the career which was all she had had, or
wanted, since Hugh Hamilton had regretfully returned
her to store and married his heiress. She made a decision.

'Look, I'm tired,' she said to their guests with her
charming smile. 'I guess the height must have got to me
after all. It wouldn't spoil your evening if you spend the
rest of it without me, would it?' she asked with just the
faintest touch of irony.

The Ministry men were all smiles; politely regretful but nevertheless relieved. Her presence had exerted an inhibiting effect on their efforts to enjoy themselves at the expense of the North American company. Now, their expressions said clearly, they would be able to get down to it seriously.

She said to Larry rapidly, 'I'll take care of the bill up to now. You handle the rest. And I'll use the car if that's OK with you.'

The President, before he realised that Technica Associates was not going to oblige him in the matter of a Swiss bank account, had placed a chauffeured limousine at the disposal of Señorita Lennox and her assistant.

'You go ahead, I'll take a cab,' said Larry, adding with his boyish grin, 'Good job I packed. I can see these boys want to make a night of it. I wouldn't be surprised if I just pick up my suitcases and drive straight on to the plane tomorrow morning.'

Julia smiled. 'I'll keep a seat for you. You'll deserve it.'

And she stood up, smiling farewells at their guests, begging them not to leave their seats as a waiter approached with another tray of drinks. On her way out she paused by the desk and asked for the bill for table twenty-four. It raised eyebrows but they were too sophisticated to demur. She barely glanced at it before pushing her credit card across the desk.

'I'll collect my cloak. Would you have them call my car, please. The name is Lennox.'

The girl on the desk exchanged glances with the bowing waiter. Julia noticed it, but dismissed it as irrelevant at the time. She was genuinely tired now, weariness submerging that prickling instinct for impending disaster that she had had all evening. She combed her hair, retrieved her long black satin cloak, tipped the girl in the cloakroom and came out to sign her credit card and take her receipt.

Her driver was standing by the bank of flowers at the

door, turning his peaked cap in his fingers. He looked faintly nervous. He jumped to open the glass doors for her and then darted ahead to open the back door of the limousine. The road was still in darkness. The power cut had obviously taken out all the street lighting and there was no traffic on the road.

Julia sat back in the luxurious cushions as he closed the door on her. The inside of the limousine smelled of leather and cigar smoke and expensive masculine cologne—and something else, something sweetish and faintly nauseating. She made a face. Oh well, it was only a ten-minute drive back to her hotel, she would just have to hold her breath.

The driver slid into the front seat. He seemed to be hunched, as if he were cold. Julia noticed it idly. He made a mess of turning the engine on, too. Twice the car stalled and, when he finally had the engine running, the car shot forward and had to be braked hard.

He must have been drinking, Julia thought, as she bounced forward and back on the deep upholstery. That was the only thing that could account for the change. He had seemed an admirable driver earlier.

Even as she was puzzling over it, the car slewed to the left across the road and there was a hideous scream of brakes. There were lights everywhere, dazzling her. The limousine thudded into something—Julia thought it was another car—and then bumped drunkenly along until it came to rest at a crazy angle. She was flung to the floor.

The offside door was wrenched open. She heard voices, loud voices, filled with fear or excitement. She struggled to get up but she was winded, and anyway, the intruders gave her no time. Something black was thrown over her face and the sweetish smell became overpowering.

At last Julia recognised it. Chloroform, she thought, clawing at the thing covering her face and subsiding, terrified, into violent unconsciousness.

When she came to herself it was daylight. The first thing she saw was a sliver of light through a chink of material. What was it, a curtain? She tried to turn her head to see better, and at the sharp pain behind her eyes, desisted. No, it was not a curtain, it was a blindfold. Somebody had drugged her and probably hit her and blindfolded her, and she had no idea where she was.

She lay very still, trying to make sense of it.

There was no sense of motion, so she was not in a car, or if she was, it was not moving. There was no sound of engines either. In the distance she thought she could hear voices. She had a sudden, sharp sense of being alone. She held her breath, painfully, for her chest hurt, and there was no sound at all, no other body breathing.

She moved a little, stretched. Her hands were tied at the wrists, quite loosely. Her ankles were free. Whatever she was lying on was hard. She moved again and something fell, with a noise like thunder. The voices in the distance stopped.

A door opened; she heard the creak of its hinge behind her head.

A girl's voice said in Spanish, 'She's awake. What are we going to do?'

There was a muttered answer, that Julia could not catch. Then hands were on her, clumsy but not rough, and she was edged upright. Her head swam and a sudden awful possibility presented itself to her.

She said in her precise Spanish, 'I am very sorry, but I am going to be sick.'

The girl made a wordless exclamation and whipped the muffling blindfold away from Julia's face just in time. Some sort of tin basin was thrust at her which she could not hold because her hands were tied behind her back. She was violently sick.

When it was over she sagged back, shaking. She was

drenched in sweat but she felt very cold. The girl eyed her
doubtfully.

'Are you all right?'

Julia managed a pale smile. 'I don't know.'

'Are you ill in some way: I mean a heart condition, or
anything?'

She shook her head.

'Thank God for that! At least the imbeciles have not
brought us an invalid.' The girl sounded suddenly savage.

Julia tried to collect herself. 'Where—where am I?'

At once the girl's face tightened. She did not answer.

'I'm not still in Alto Rio, am I?' asked Julia, some
vague memories of a night of frightening speed and
silence returning to her.

'You will be told. If it is necessary for you to know.'

'Oh.' Julia digested this thoughtfully. She still felt
ghastly, but her powers of deduction were returning to
her. 'Is this a kidnap?'

The question seemed to make the girl uneasy. Julia
could not see the reason that it should do so, since they
had already bound and blindfolded her. Or perhaps they
had exceeded their instructions, and the girl was not sure
that they should have bound and blindfolded her. She
decided on an experiment.

'My arms ache. Do you think you could cut me loose?'

The girl seemed undecided. Then she nodded and
came forward, a serviceable penknife in her hand. She
dealt with Julia's bonds very efficiently. Julia hoped that
her eyes had not widened at the sight of the weapon or
the efficiency; she did not think it would be politic to let
herself seem afraid. For the moment she was not going to
think about whether she was afraid or not; the
appearance of courage was quite enough to handle.

'Thank you,' she said, flexing her cramped shoulders.

'It is nothing.' The girl hesitated. 'We have a little time
to wait, maybe not long, Do you want some coffee?'

Julia wondered briefly whether it would be drugged

and decided to risk it. She needed something to remove the vile taste in her mouth.

'Yes, please.'

'Then I will fetch you some. Stay here, please.' The girl gave her a long, measuring look. 'I do not need to tell you not to move, do I, *señorita*? We do not want to hurt you, but we are very serious people.'

Julia swallowed. She found the girl's quiet words more impressive than any threats would have been. She nodded. The girl went out.

She was gone so long Julia thought she had forgotten coffee, forgotten her prisoner. Julia looked round her prison. It was a long thin room, with a window on either side covered by Venetian blinds. There was a tall filing cabinet in one corner and on the end wall a huge map was pinned. It looked like a wartime operations room, she thought smiling faintly.

And then the smile died. For that must be exactly what it was, she realised. She'd heard of the local guerrilla activity, but Technica's information department said that it was only small local groups and confined to the mountains. She and Larry would not be bothered by it in any way.

Julia caught her breath in a smothered groan that was half a laugh. Bothered! She rotated her wrists. The raw rope had chafed them and they ached because she had been lying on them. She felt sick, and she did not know where she was. She would tell Tony to fire the entire Information Department the moment she got back, she promised herself.

There was an impatient step outside. Voices rose as if several people were trying to shout each other down, then there was a loud bang, as if a heavy piece of furniture had been kicked over. The voice quieted. Words became audible.

'. . . *no* common sense at all!' It was a voice that cracked like a whip. Instinctively Julia flinched. She felt quite sorry for whoever was getting this tongue lashing. At the same time she was anxious not to face what was evidently a very angry man herself.

'We followed orders.' Another voice, younger, very stiff. 'To the letter.'

'You were not ordered to capture a *woman*!' the other said sharply.

A girl's voice interposed. It sounded as if she were soothing them. It also sounded like the girl Julia had met. 'We were told to take this Lennox, and this we have done.'

'You have not. You acted too early. Lennox was still in the club when you jumped that woman's car—and made a God-awful noise in doing it. They had the army out in half an hour. Do you know *that*? Did you think of that when you started playing Hercules?'

'It was unfortunate . . .' the girl allowed but was interrupted.

'It was more than unfortunate—it was bloody stupid! And it was a disaster. It meant I could do nothing to rectify the situation while you clattered off out of town with your prisoner.' The voice was filled with scorn.

'That Gregorio was to blame,' the younger voice said sulkily. 'He was so scared, he could not hold the car straight.'

'Then you should have got rid of him and driven the car yourself.'

'But they already knew him,' the boy objected.

'People like that don't take any notice of chauffeurs. They would not have known or cared who was driving them. You are a fool, Pepe,' but he sounded weary now. His fury seemed to have spent itself. 'I'd better see her when she comes round.'

'She is conscious,' said the girl. She paused and then added expressionlessly, 'She was not very well.'

This was greeted with a bark of humourless laughter. 'Did she throw up? You should have thought of that when you filled her full of chloroform!'

'She seems to be recovering,' snapped the younger voice, identified as Pepe. 'She is asking for coffee.'

'Good, then you shall bring her some. Bring some for me too.'

Julia sank back on to her hard couch as there came the unmistakable sounds of approaching footsteps. She tried to compose herself, compressing her mouth into a tight line to prevent its trembling and folding her shaking hands tightly together. He should not see how afraid she was.

The door opened, and she stared in amazement so great that she forgot her terror. Don Roberto Madariaga stood there. Julia gaped at him.

It was evident that he did not share her surprise. His face was tight and angry but there was no hint of surprise. He had known whom he would see when he opened that door. Julia began to feel indignation welling up inside her.

She said pleasantly, 'Good morning, *señor.*'

If anything he looked even angrier at her greeting. He shut the door behind him with a vicious movement and came towards her.

'What have those stupid children done to you?'

'What you told them to, I imagine,' she said coolly, meeting his eyes full on.

'I did not tell them to turn you into a ghost.' His voice was harsh.

She allowed herself a satirical smile. 'Or to drug me? Or to kidnap me?'

'Kidnap, yes,' he said, equally coolly. 'Though not you. You, I must tell you frankly, are a complication—an unwelcome complication. And the chloroform,' he sounded disgusted, 'was a refinement of their own. God knows where they got it. They don't seem to have had much idea of how to use it. The jeep reeks of the stuff. I imagine the Presidential car must also do so.'

'How clumsy of them,' she said sweetly.

'Unnecessary, at least.' He seemed to have recovered his temper somewhat. He sat on the edge of the desk facing her, swinging one booted foot. Julia realised with a start how very different he looked this morning.

Last night, in dinner jacket and crisp white shirt he had been attractive. This morning he was devastating. He was wearing dark denims and a safari jacket, both creased. There was a dark line of stubble on his jaw that showed clearly that though he might have taken time to change he had not bothered to shave. His eyes were weary and his beautiful long-fingered hands were marked with oil or grease. And he was still devastating; even furious and faintly sick, Julia could feel the magnetism of the man. It made her even angrier.

He was speaking ruefully. 'They were supposed to get your companion, the leader of the mission, Julio Lennox.'

There was a little silence. Then Julia said carefully, 'You seem to have given them conflicting information. You can hardly blame them.'

The strange hazel eyes lifted, inspected her.

'What do you mean?' Madariaga asked softly.

She gave him a small smile. 'That you should have told them to get either my companion or Lennox. I am the leader of the mission—Julia Lennox.'

Shock washed through him; she saw it in the uncontrolled flaring of his eyes, the immediately suppressed clenching of his hands. But at once he had himself in hand again.

'I do not believe that they would send a woman to negotiate with President Valetta.'

'I assure you they did!' She was offended. 'And he was getting first-class treatment. I've been a director of Technica since it started, but up to now I've dealt mainly with the African continent. It was only because I have just been transferred to Latin America that I came myself. It was a sort of familiarisation trip. Normally, Larry would have handled the negotiations, and I would only have come down for the signing of the agreement.'

The handsome head shook slowly, not as if he did not believe her but as though he were trying to assimilate this new and unwelcome information.

'We were certainly looking for a director. That was why we picked Technica rather than one of the other foreign companies. But—a *woman*?' He shut his eyes. 'Do you know I have some of this country's best brains working for me gathering information?'

His tone of despair would have been comic in other circumstances. As it was, Julia could not laugh. She was beginning to shake convulsively, either with reaction to the drug or the emotional strain. She did her best to disguise it, but it was not easy when her teeth were all but chattering.

'Perhaps you should have specified, told them that a woman would not do,' she snapped.

Madariaga gave her a long look. 'Perhaps I should, but it is too late now. Your associate has no doubt left the country and you are here. I shall have to change my plans.'

Julia felt sick. His look was cold, appraising.

She spoke quickly. 'Technica Associates won't pay ransom, you know. It's part of their public policy. They work all over the world in countries with political troubles and they can't afford for there to be any doubt about it.'

He seemed unperturbed. 'Not even for a director? I am told—but then my information is sloppy, that could be wrong—a *key* director?'

Julia shook her head. 'Not even for a key director.' She smiled bleakly. 'Particularly not one who helped to agree the no-ransom policy in the first place.'

'But your family? Would they not apply pressure?'

Julia swallowed. This was not something that hurt

normally. She was used to being on her own; she even
liked it. It gave her freedom. There was nobody to
consult in her decisions except herself. It meant that she
could take all sorts of chances that would not have been
fair to a family, to people who loved her. And Julia was a
gambler. She liked taking risks.

But now she felt horribly lonely.

She said, hoping the desolation did not show in her
voice, 'No family.'

'No?' He received the information without emotion,
though she thought he gave her a curious look. He shifted
on his desk corner. 'Well, honesty compels me to tell you
that I did not really contemplate ransoming you anyway,
señorita.' He saw stark fear flare in her eyes and added
roughly, 'Nor anything violent, either, you need not fear.
Dear God, do my countrymen have some such a name for
thuggery?'

It was becoming nearly impossible to control the
shaking. Julia pressed her hands together hard but
managed to say lightly, 'Well, you have to admit that
being kidnapped by Latin American guerrillas hasn't
had a very good press recently—not as the ideal way of
passing a vacation.'

He was not deceived by her flippancy. She thought she
saw sympathy flicker in his face for a moment, then it
was expressionless again.

'I see I shall have to give you a brief lesson in modern
history.' He stood up and looked down at her a little
mockingly. 'How much do you know about my country,
Señorita Lennox?'

Julia took that with composure. 'Eight million people,
two high-density population centres, but the majority are
rural farmers on subsistence agriculture. Mountainous
hinterland and low-lying coastal strip subject to floods.
Fertile soil but uncertain rainfall and irregular watercourses makes agriculture precarious.'

Madariaga was taken aback. She saw it and was

pleased, in spite of her fears.

'I'm an agronomist,' she told him softly.

'Among other things.' For a moment he looked horribly grim.

'Who wanted to sell your President an irrigation project.' Her voice grew wistful. 'It was a good project.'

He misunderstood her. 'Don't worry, he may still buy it. Or someone will. God knows, the Highlands need something. They've been neglected for years.'

As this was exactly Julia's view she said nothing. Her finely marked brows met in a frown. She did not understand this man. He seemed too cool, too unimpassioned to be one of the freedom fighters she had seen on televised news—yet the piratical way she had been seized and her indubitable imprisonment suggested that that was exactly what he was.

He was saying, 'You are well informed on the geography, I give you that, *Señorita* Lennox. But history was what I was talking about.'

She said, 'Military government in power for the last four years. That's all I know.'

'Yes.' Madariaga said it heavily. 'Yes, I expect that's all most of the outside world knows.' His glance flitted over her briefly. Julia had the impression that he was not seeing her but somebody else, somebody who caused his beautiful mouth to tighten in remembered pain. 'It's not quite as simple as that.'

He turned away from her, his hands stuffed in the pocket of his jeans. His back was stiff with tension, she saw suddenly, almost as if he was as nervous as she was.

'The truth is that for years Oaxacan was only nominally a country. It was effectively run as a series of private estates by wealthy families. On the whole,' he added reflectively, 'not badly run.' His voice grew bitter. 'At least nobody starved.'

Julia frowned. 'So what happened? I thought the ecological balance was stable in this area. Was there a population explosion or something?'

'No.' He sounded faintly amused. 'No, we're under-populated anyway and the birth rate is not high. No, it's quite simply a question of bad administration—years and years of it. The great families became enlightened, you see, and saw the error of their ways. All the Oxford and Sorbonne-educated sons came home and said there had to be democracy, an elected government, universal franchise.' He flung his hands up in the air. 'It was chaos!'

Julia was rather shocked. 'Don't you believe in democracy?'

'In theory.' He swung round on her, his mouth smiling, his eyes bitter. 'Just as in theory I believe in food and shelter and a decent way of life for the whole world. The trouble is bringing it about.'

She was shaken. 'So what happened?'

Suddenly Madariaga looked tired. 'Oh, it was no different from dozens of other little places, I suppose. All the big brothers of the world started to take an interest in the emerging nation. They probably meant well. But we have ninety per cent illiteracy here and the finer points of political argument don't mean much to isolated mountain villagers. They divide on family lines: very ancient families, almost tribes. None of us appreciated that, not the outsiders, nor the ruling classes, not even the villagers themselves.'

'And?' prompted Julia, as he fell into frowning silence.

He stirred. 'The Marxists got to some, the Trotskyists to others. There were various right-wing factions that moved in, mainly in the south. Going down the highway between here and Alto Rio you could pass through as many as seven different guerrilla areas. Travel became impossible, violence a daily event. The one thing, of course, that the big brothers had supplied in quantity was arms. We had twenty years of civil war.'

Julia was appalled. 'I had no idea!'

He shrugged. 'Sometimes there was a government for a few months that controlled enough of the country to get a few things done: some roads repaired, that sort of thing. And then there would be another revolution and the fighting would start all over again, town against country, village against village, coast against highlands. There is a whole generation in my country that cannot remember a time of peace, Señorita Lennox.'

'But the military government—surely it's been there for four years, not just a few months,' Julia protested.

His smile was wry. 'That shows how little you know about my country, *señorita*. The military have controlled the two cities you so admirably described to me just now. That is all. The capital and the port, that is where they have their barracks. It means to a certain extent that they can control foreign trade—what there is of it. But the rest of the country: no. There is still fighting. They do not even attempt to control it, on the whole. The people just fight among themselves.'

'Including you?' asked Julia, taking her courage in both hands.

'Me?' He seemed as if he did not understand her.

She gestured round the room. 'All of this. Is it not the headquarters of just another guerrilla faction?'

This time she recognised the silence as dangerous. Those hazel eyes narrowed to slits. At last he said softly, 'You are very brave, *señorita*, brave and reckless.'

'In what way?' asked Julia, feeling less brave by the minute.

'You know nothing of the history, the politics, of this country and yet you dare to say such a thing to me!' His voice was very quiet, not much above a whisper, but she could feel the fury licking through it like subterranean fire.

She ran her tongue nervously over her lips. His eyes flickered at the movement.

She said, 'Why have you brought me here? What are

you going to do with me?'

His eyes still on her lips, Madariaga said harshly, 'I am beginning to ask myself that question.'

Julia felt fear, real cold fear such as she had never experienced in her life, begin to seep into her. It was not a reasoning emotion. She had known all along that she was in the power of this man and his associates, that she would have to walk carefully and talk sweetly. But she had forgotten to be conciliating. Something about him, the way he talked or the way he looked or his general manner, had made her forget that he was her captor, with the power of life or death over her. Indeed, for a few moments she had forgotten she was his prisoner. She had responded to him as if they were newly introduced, in ordinary surroundings; as if they might one day become friends.

Now, as the fear crept through her shrinking body, she realised they could never be friends. He was too much of a threat. Julia felt as if she were in the presence of some unstable chemical that might explode. Wryly she acknowledged to herself that she felt as if it were her presence that might cause that explosion. He had not been violent, hardly even hostile. It was she who had provoked him.

Helplessly she met his eyes, struggling for composure.

'What do you intend to do with me?' she whispered, cold with fear.

'You? Well, I have had several plans in the last twenty-four hours. Originally, I intended to trade Señor Lennox to the President in return for certain concessions.'

'Why can't you trade Señorita Lennox, then?' asked Julia as calmly as she could.

'I thought it—unchivalrous.' Madariaga laughed harshly. 'Or, if you understand it better, Señorita Lennox, I thought it was too downmarket to make use of a woman for such a purpose. You will laugh, but I had intended to return you to Alto Rio this morning.'

Julia was very pale. She did not misunderstand his insults. They hurt, surprisingly fiercely.

But she concentrated on the most important word among the insults. 'Had?'

'Had, Señorita Lennox,' he repeated softly. 'You have convinced me that I must be less—sexist—in my outlook.' The cold eyes were mocking. 'You would not want any special concessions to your sex, I am sure. And I find it—shall we say, convenient? Yes, on reflection I find it convenient to keep you here and send my message to the General after all.'

She said, 'And if he doesn't agree to your concessions?'

'Then you and I will have to have a serious talk as to what else you might be able to contribute to my operation.' He sounded almost bored, but Julia was not deceived.

'You've got some plan, haven't you?' she demanded, shaky but determined.

'Plan?'

'For me.'

'Ah, for you.' He smiled slowly. 'How very perceptive of you!'

'Tell me.'

His mouth twisted into a private smile that Julia did not like at all.

'You can't expect me to tell you all my contingency plans, Señorita Lennox. I have been very straightforward with you, but you must allow me one or two secrets.'

She whispered, 'What do you mean?'

Madariaga was leaving. For a moment she thought he would not answer. But at the door he turned back and looked her over coolly.

'Just that—if the General does not want to trade, or not to trade immediately——' he paused and the smile grew, making her tremble, 'I can think of a way that you might make yourself useful.'

'Useful?' It was not what she had expected. It had an

oddly workaday sound, as if he wanted her to do housework or type his letters for him. She frowned, not quite daring to be reassured. 'Useful to—' she gestured to the map at the end of the room and echoed his own words, 'useful to your operation?'

The smile grew. 'Useful to me,' he corrected gently. And was gone.

CHAPTER THREE

WHEN he had gone the coffee came at last. It was very hot and black and had already been sugared. Julia cupped her hands round the tiny cup, warming them. She did not take sugar in her coffee and she found the brew undrinkable after the first sip.

The girl who brought it watched her, frowning.

'Do you still feel—unwell?'

Julia shook her head. 'No. But I'm very cold.'

The girl sniffed. 'You are not dressed for the mountains,' she said in a neutral voice.

Julia forbore to say that she had not intended to visit the mountains. Instead she nodded in agreement and remarked, 'I had a cloak with me last night. Did it get lost?'

The girl shook her head. She went to the end of Julia's couch and picked up a squashy black bundle from the floor. It was the satin cloak.

'This will not keep you warm,' she said, extending it to Julia. She stroked her hand across the black stuff almost wistfully. 'It is very pretty. My sister would like it.'

Julia sipped at the coffee again. It was probably a good thing to keep the girl talking. She might even glean some useful information from her. She gave her a small smile.

'How old is your sister?'

In answer the girl's look was ironic. 'My sister is not a child, señorita, just because she likes pretty things. She is the dancer Florita—I believe you saw her last night.'

Julia considered the news carefully. The girl looked nothing like the beautiful dancer. Her hair was mousy, where Florita's was tawny and in her creased jeans she was stocky and ungraceful. Still, sisters were often not

40

alike and they might nevertheless be very fond of each other.

She said, 'Does your sister share your views? Your way of life?'

The other girl smiled. 'You won't see her in a mountain village breaking her nails at a weaving loom, if that's what you mean, *señorita*. On the other hand, she and Roberto work very closely. They planned last night's operation together.'

Julia remembered her feeling that Roberto and the dancer had been putting on some kind of performance. She gave a little shiver. She would never ignore her instincts again, she promised herself.

The girl went on proudly, 'Florita is very famous, very popular. Roberto often says that he does not know what he would do without her.'

'I'm sure he doesn't,' murmured Julia wryly. She shrugged the black satin cloak round herself.

'You look cold,' the girl said with compunction. 'When we get to—that is, when we arrive, I will find some jeans and a warm shirt for you.'

'Thank you,' said Julia trying to hide her dismay. So they were taking her somewhere else; presumably somewhere even further from the capital. 'Er—will it be long?'

The girl gave her a sharp look. 'Who knows?' she said evasively, clearly deciding that she had already bandied too many words with her prisoner. 'And it would be better for you, *señorita*, not to ask. Roberto is not in a good mood. It would be better not to anger him further.'

Julia shrugged. 'The only thing I've done to anger him is turn out not to be a man,' she pointed out with some justice. 'That's hardly my fault.'

The girl looked surprised. 'Oh, but you made him very angry, *señorita*. I do not know what you said to him, but whatever it was you put him into a rage.' A certain respect crept into her voice. 'It is not easy to make

Roberto lose his temper, either. Normally he is completely the advocate, very calm and sensible.' She gave a grin
which suddenly made her look much younger. 'It can be
very annoying.'

'You've known him a long time?' Julia asked.

'All my life,' the girl said simply. 'He is like a brother.
Perhaps one day he will be my brother—it is what my
mother always hoped. But when Florita started dancing
my mother said it was not a respectable profession for the
wife of a public man and that now Roberto would never
marry her.' She frowned, as if suddenly recalling that this
was gossip and Julia was the enemy. 'But this can be of
no interest to you, *señorita*. And I must go and prepare for
the journey.'

When she had gone, Julia stood up, stretching her
cramped limbs. She found her legs were not steady and
she felt slightly light-headed, as if she was recovering
from a long illness. She went to the window and peered
out but the view did not tell her much.

She seemed to be in a shack by the side of an
unmetalled road. There were two cars and a medium
sized truck parked at angles to the building, but she could
see no signs of life. Beyond the road were tangled clumps
of bushes, thick but not very high, which effectively
blocked any view of the landscape. The sky was a
cloudless blue.

She huddled the cloak round her. Her evening dress
was as thin as it was pretty. She thought ruefully of the
packed case full of tweed skirts and jackets that she had
left in the hotel. What would happen to it? Would Larry
take it to the airport with him, believing that she would
follow? Or would the hotel impound it? After all she had
not yet paid her bill.

She bit her lip, wondering what Tony would have to
say about the situation. Normally he was very impatient
with anything that interrupted the smooth flow of
Technica's success. Tony's view was that people who got

themselves kidnapped had generally been indiscreet or, worse, careless, and did not deserve to be ransomed, even if their companies could afford it.

Julia sighed. She did not think she had been careless.

The door banged open, startling her. It was a young man, one she had not seen before. His eyes were very bright and he looked at her with dislike but when he spoke, it was politely enough.

'You are to come with me, Señorita Lennox. Now, if you please.'

Julia felt her heart give a lurch of panic and quelled the feeling. She had to keep her wits about her. And this was a boy. Roberto Madariaga might be a dangerously intelligent enemy, but she was too self-controlled to break out in a sweat of fear because a boy looked at her with hostility—or so she told herself.

She said meekly, 'Very well. But could I—er—wash first?'

For a moment he looked uncomprehending, then a dark flush burnt into his cheek.

'Of course,' he said stiffly. 'Marta will show you where. Please to be quick.'

Marta was already geared up to leave. She had added a thick woven poncho over her trousers and was toting a serviceable duffle bag. The room itself, which Julia had not glimpsed when she was brought in originally, was a sort of primitive café. There were three scrubbed wooden tables and some rickety chairs as well as a corner bar. Behind the bar was a large woman, with her hair hidden under her scarf and a flash of gold teeth every time she smiled. She smiled at Julia and gestured to a door at the far side of the room, but she looked worried.

They all looked worried, thought Julia, as she rinsed her hands and then for good measure, splashed some of the cold water on her face and wrists. The woman in the café, Florita last night, the chauffeur; all of them except Roberto Madariaga.

Julia considered that for a long time. She sat quietly in the jeep, next first to the boy, Pepe, and later, when he took over driving the truck and disappeared at a fork in the road, to Marta. They were all tense except for Madariaga. Was that because he had more nerve? Or because he had less to lose? These were the guerrillas, after all, out in the countryside and, apparently, on the windy side of the authorities. While Madariaga walked free in Alto Rio, able to stroll into the city's most expensive nightclub without question. Yet Marta spoke of him without resentment, even with affection.

The girl drove without speaking. It was not an unfriendly silence. She was concentrating on the road, and Julia could understand that: it was pitted with large potholes and enormous ridges where tyres of heavy vehicles must have passed during the rains.

Julia observed the route she took carefully. Already she was beginning to think of ways she might escape and to know the road back would be essential. She did not think it would be very difficult. They were climbing steadily and, though the road was occasionally joined by small pathways, the only road big enough to take a vehicle was that on to which Pepe had taken the truck.

They did not see anybody. The road did not pass through any hamlets and, though Julia could occasionally make out what appeared to be cultivated fields behind the bushes that lined the road, there was nobody working in them. She wondered bleakly if the villagers fled at the sound of a motor engine.

Eventually they turned off the road on to what looked like a crumbled wall of pebble. Julia gasped as the jeep lurched, swung round and then surged forwards up the stony track. She grasped the door handle to steady herself, and Marta cast her a quick unsmiling glance.

'Do not try to run away, señorita. This is our home territory—no one would help you.'

'I'll bear it in mind,' said Julia, wincing as the jeep's

nose rose at an almost impossible angle to take the next bend.

'While you are with us, we will do our best to make you comfortable,' Marta went on. 'I do not think it will be for long.'

Julia had no answer for that. She was too intent on hanging on to the side of the jeep lest she be forcibly ejected from it at one of the steep, vicious bends which Marta took without a blink.

'You may find much to interest you,' the cool little voice went on. 'There are ruins behind the village. And the local crafts are still pursued.'

'What a shame I didn't bring my camera,' said Julia with irony.

The girl sniffed and said no more. There was little doubt that, though she was civil enough, she thought her prisoner was a poor thing, Julia thought ruefully. And by the time they finally reached the village, she looked a poor thing indeed. She was feeling sick again and when she got stiffly out of the jeep, she swayed.

'It is the altitude,' somebody said in an unsurprised but not unfriendly tone.

And that was the last Julia remembered before she fainted.

This time she did not awake bound and alone. She came to slowly, hearing a fuzz of voices above her and feeling a delicious warmth creeping slowly into her chilled bones.

'Ah, poor thing, she is coming round,' said a voice she did not recognise in strongly accented Spanish.

She opened her eyes cautiously. A woman was bending over her, tucking some sort of blanket round her shoulders, patting her shoulder encouragingly.

'You will feel better in a moment, child.'

Julia believed her. For a moment her lashes drifted down again and then flew open. She struggled up on to her elbow. The woman made clucking noises, urging her to lie down again.

'Hush! Lie down and get your strength back. You have had a bad time and you are not yet acclimatised to the height,' the woman said solicitously.

Julia stared at her wildly, only half understanding. Then, seeing the kindness and evident concern in the lined face, she did what she had not done for years, and began to cry.

At once the woman sat down on the edge of her couch and took her into her arms, patting her heaving shoulders as if she was a child.

'There, there, don't take on. It's all over now—you're safe now.' She turned her head and addressed someone standing in the darkness behind her. 'Poor child, she's frozen! Don Roberto should be ashamed of himself. He is not a silly stripling like that Pepe. He should have more respect for his name, if not for himself. What Doña Eleanora would have said, I hate to think. Poor child, poor child—there, there!'

Julia, who could never remember being called a poor child before, allowed herself the luxury of weeping on the sympathetic shoulder for some few minutes. All the time the woman kept up her consolatory monologue, with angry asides over her shoulder. Eventually Julia drew a long breath, rubbed her knuckles over her red eyelids, and sat up, pushing the hair out of her face. Her comforter smiled at her.

'You feel better now, yes?' She patted Julia's face.

Julia gulped and nodded.

'Good. Marta has gone to get you some of her clothes, so you will be more comfortable. And I, Angelina, will make you a hot drink I give my grandchildren for the altitude sickness.' She stood up. 'But do not move too quickly or too suddenly. Not until you have got used to the height.' She gave her a gap-toothed smile. 'When you go back to your own grandmother, you shall tell her how well I take care of you.'

She went, followed by the woman who had been standing in the shadows behind her. Julia could not make out who it was, though she thought the woman was younger than Angelina, perhaps a daughter or even a granddaughter, since family ties seemed to pervade everything here.

She leaned back, her hands behind her tumbled hair. It was all so alien to her, this emphasis on families. She could not remember her mother; she had never known her father. If she had grandparents living, she did not know who they were or where to find them.

Julia reflected wryly on her childhood. Uncle Geoffrey had not wanted her and made no secret of the fact. He had bitterly resented it when the Children's Officer had told him that Julia would not be taken into a children's home as long as she had a living relative financially able to support her. She could still remember vividly standing in the cold kitchen, not understanding what was happening while Uncle Geoffrey shouted at the Children's Officer, 'If my wife and I had wanted children we would have had them, and not an ugly little brat like that!'

Julia shifted slightly. It did not hurt any more. It had never really *hurt*, not the way it hurt if you were betrayed by someone you loved and trusted. She had never liked Uncle Geoffrey, any more than he liked her. She had learned to keep quiet and out of the way. She had become a very self-contained child, disguising both the strong will and that hint of recklessness that she had inherited from her mother.

It was her strength of will that had, against the odds and Uncle Geoffrey's disclaimer of all responsibility, got her to university. She had kept herself there by a succession of spare-time jobs, which paid the rent and bought her the books she needed. She had looked like a scarecrow, of course.

In the darkness, Julia smiled at the memories of her

younger self, determined, earnest and generally wrapped
in several sweaters against the cold because she could not
afford to run her small electric fire. God, she had been
poor! Most of her Manhattan colleagues would not
believe how poor she had been in Glasgow. And she had
been so happy, free for the first time from Uncle
Geoffrey and utterly absorbed by her research.

Hugh had laughed at her for her passion for her work.
Julia shifted again and this time stopped smiling. Hugh
Hamilton's betrayal did hurt. Even now, nearly ten years
later, independent, self-sufficient snd successful though
she was, Julia could turn icy at the memory of Hugh
Hamilton and the younger self who had thought she was
in love.

She gave herself a mental shake. Why should she be
thinking of Hugh now? He was married years ago, to the
girl from across the glen who had come from the same
background as himself and understood him. Hugh had
explained that carefully to a white-faced Julia, shocked
awake out of her afternoon doze of love by the intrusion
and departure of his Caroline.

'Don't worry,' he had said soothingly. 'Caro knows it
doesn't mean anything. Don't look so stricken, my
mouse.'

But of course she had been stricken, stricken to the
heart. Hugh's Caroline might know that it meant nothing
for Hugh to take a thin, serious graduate student to his
bed on an otherwise boring afternoon. Hugh was a young
and popular tutor; Caroline probably thought it was no
more than she need expect and had been prepared to
settle for when she agreed to marry him.

The trouble was that it was not what Julia expected.
She had had a cold rather than a strict upbringing, and
perhaps because of that she had poured out all her stored
up love on Hugh Hamilton's unsuspecting head. When
he wanted to make love to her it had been her delight to
give him everything he wanted without stinting.

In retrospect, Julia realised that Hugh had been surprised and touched by her ardour. He had called her his mouse. He had been carelessly affectionate. And— when he could persuade her away from the laboratory or her books, which was not as often as he liked—he had been her lover. It had never occurred to Julia that he was not as much in love as she was. It had never crossed her mind that he might already be engaged to a suitable heiress, the date for their wedding already set.

After Caroline left that afternoon, Hugh had explained. He thought Julia knew all about his engagement. Everybody did; it had been in all the forthcoming marriages columns. It was beyond his comprehension that Julia did not even know such columns were printed in newspapers, much less read them.

All the long lonely years of self-containment had stepped in to help Julia through that black afternoon. While Hugh assured her, smiling, that she need not fear that she had ruined his engagement, Julia had composedly climbed back into her clothes, saying nothing. She did not tell him that the only life she was afraid she had ruined by her incautious affection was her own.

In the end, in spite of his bland self-absorption, Hugh must have noticed something in her brief replies to his assurances. He had put a careless arm round her tense shoulders and given her a friendly squeeze.

'You're a funny little thing, my mouse. But honestly, you don't need to worry about Caro. She's a good sort, she won't make a fuss.'

It was fortunate, Julia thought grimly, that Hugh had never realised just how far from being a good sort she was herself. If she had been less hurt, she would have made the fuss of the century. But as it was, she was mortally hurt. All she wanted to do was to get away from him and from the dreams of a golden, loving future that she had not even realised she was dreaming until Caroline had

interrupted them and Hugh had made it plain that his
future lay elsewhere.

Well, the future had been very different from anything
she had envisaged. After she got her degree she turned
down all the offers of teaching posts in England and
Scotland. Hugh had been faintly puzzled. She still had to
see him, of course, he was her supervisor. He had
accepted philosophically her refusal to sleep with him
after Caroline's intrusion, though there was little chance
that he understood it. But he remained, to Julia's private
pain, friendly, eager to help her career. He had been
slightly offended when she was not overwhelmed by the
offers of work that, he claimed, he had engineered for
her.

'I'm going to the States,' Julia had told him in her soft
voice.

'The *States*?' Hugh had not believed it. 'Have you got a
place?'

'Not to study—to travel, to see it. To see what's going
on outside my small corner of the globe.'

'No security?' asked Hugh disapprovingly, not realising that he had been the only security Julia had ever
thought she could count on and that when he let her down
she stopped looking to be secure.

'No. Just for the fun of it,' Julia told him mockingly.

And it had been fun. She ran the back of her hand over
her clammy brow, as she remembered. It had been the
greatest fun. She liked her work: she liked helping people
make things grow, she liked solving problems, she liked
travelling and living in all sorts of styles in all sorts of
places. She had her luxury apartment in Manhattan but
she was probably only there ten or twelve weeks a year.
The rest of the time she was either talking to officials in
the exotic capitals of the developing world or she was out
on site doing field work. She was fascinated by field
work. Just as she would be fascinated, when she felt

steadier, to look round this village and what was grown here.

She was thinking in anticipation of what she might find when she realised that she must have slept. The hut was still dark but the doorway no longer showed a splash of light. There were sounds of people moving about outside, too. Julia turned and realised that someone had set an earthenware mug of something pungent at her elbow. It was lukewarm now but she suspected that it had been piping hot when it was placed beside her.

Ashamed, she quaffed it and then swung her legs to the floor and went to the door. An extraordinary sight met her eyes.

It was quite dark. There were lights in the little houses and every door stood open. There was just the one, steeply curved street, unpaved of course. Old women were sitting on hard upright chairs to one side of their doorways, while the rest of the population—old men, boys, young women, cats, dogs and chickens—was strolling about in the rock-strewn space between the two rows of houses. A quiet buzz of conversation filled the air.

Julia watched, bracing herself against the door lintel with one hand. There was no light behind her, so they did not immediately become aware of her. It was a warm, friendly sight, and perhaps because of her unhappy thoughts earlier, it moved her.

'Señorita Lennox?' It was a grave Marta, standing quietly at her elbow. 'I have brought you some clothes. They are Florita's—I am too short, I think, for my clothes to fit you, but Florita is taller than I. Though,' she added with a hint of purely feminine mischief in her voice, 'not so big in other areas. The blouse is mine. I hope they fit.'

'Thank you,' said Julia, receiving them gratefully. 'I was wondering what I ought to do, what was expected.'

In the darkness Marta smiled at her. 'Please do whatever you would like, Señorita Lennox. This is an ordinary village. You are most welcome.'

'But—' Julia still hesitated, 'where do you want me to stay?'

The girl laughed. 'There is no town gaol where we can lock you up, if that is what you mean, *señorita*. This house is yours for as long as you need it.'

Julia frowned. 'But isn't this Angelina's house? I wouldn't want to turn her out . . .'

Marta shook her head vigorously. 'You are considerate, but no. Angelina lives in the big square house over there at the end of the village. When you have changed you may go and speak with her.'

'Then—who have I dispossessed?' asked Julia, remembering the figure she had seen hovering behind Angelina earlier.

'No one. The house is empty. It belongs to someone who inherited it but does not live here. Angelina cleans it so that it is ready, that is all.' Unexpectedly Marta put out a hand and touched Julia lightly on the arm. Her voice was warm. 'Use it with our blessing, Señorita Lennox. You have turned nobody out of doors.'

So Julia used it. It was a simple one room affair, as she discovered the next morning. It had a large family sized wooden bed in the furthest recess from the door, a simple table under the one window, several chairs and a tall chest. The walls and the stone floor were covered with beautiful rugs in natural colours. The bed was made with cotton sheets, slightly yellowed from much laundering and exquisitely starched. There was a large coverlet woven in a starburst pattern of greens, golds and turquoises. For all its simplicity it was meticulously clean. The only thing missing was cooking pots; clearly the owner, whoever it might be, did not cook when in residence.

Julia found that she did not need to cook either. Every night she ate the main meal of the day with Marta, Angelina and half a dozen others, including Angelina's ancient brother-in-law. They were friendly and outgoing, only too happy to describe their crafts and the local methods of agriculture. Only on politics they refused to be drawn.

They were quite happy to talk about the man they called Don Roberto. It soon became apparent to Julia that Angelina and, indeed, most of the village were convinced that she had been brought here because Don Roberto had no sooner set eyes on her than he had fallen madly in love with her. She protested, but they did not believe her.

She was amused by their attitude to this implied misconduct of Don Roberto's. They were faintly apologetic to Julia, as if a favourite son had raided a neighbour's orchard. For Don Roberto himself there was a disapproving shake of the head and a certain admiration. Of course, he was not a boy any more; he should have outgrown these pranks; but he was impetuous, a man of much passion, and much had to be forgiven such people.

'And,' added Angelina to Julia's acute embarrassment, 'who shall blame him when she is as beautiful as an angel?'

Julia shook her head, disclaiming. She knew she was presentable in her designer clothes, such as those she had had in her suitcase for calling on President Valetta. But in essence she had not changed from the scrawny girl with eyes too big in her thin, freckled face whom Hugh had rejected all those years ago. And in Florita's jeans her thinness was painfully obvious.

It made no difference to the romantic Angelina. And when the day came that there was the sound of an engine somewhere below the village and little Tonio came back, leaving his goats to fend for themselves, to say that Don Roberto was on his way, Angelina came bustling in to fetch Julia.

'Come quickly—come quickly! He will want to see

you,' she urged, pausing only to fluff up Julia's cloud of dark hair, before urging her out into the sunshine and towards the road up which his car would appear.

Perversely, almost as if he wanted to confirm Angelina's sentimental fancies, the first thing he said was, 'Where is she?'

Before Marta, to whom this was addressed, could answer, Angelina came forward, beaming, almost dragging the reluctant Julia after her.

'Here she is, Don Roberto. We have looked after her well for you.'

The ticked eyebrows rose and then a look of unholy amusement dawned as Madariaga took in the flushed cheeks and stormy eyes of Angelina's captive. He came forward and took her shoulders between his hands, looking down intently into her face. Behind her Julia heard Angelina give a small sigh of satisfaction. She glared at him. His smile widened.

'I can see you have, Angelina,' he said solemnly. 'She looks a different girl,' and he drew her towards him and gently kissed her forehead as if it were a benediction.

Not just Angelina, the whole village sighed sentimentally this time. Julia could have kicked him!

Marta intervened, 'Have you seen the President?'

'I have.' Madariaga was imperturbable. He took Julia's hand, threaded it into the crook of his elbow, before he strolled away from his car. She went with him perforce as he greeted friends with here a smile and there a handshake.

Marta fell into step beside them. 'And?'

'And he is thinking things over.'

She looked disappointed. 'Didn't you give him a deadline?'

'Yes.'

'When?'

'Soon enough to keep him on the hop and not so soon as to panic him,' Madariaga said coolly. 'He is going to have a very bad couple of weeks.'

'Couple of weeks!' This time it was Julia who was disappointed. 'But what about me.'

He flicked a look down at her. 'That is something we shall need to talk about. But not in public and not just at the moment, when I am tired from my drive.'

Julia withdrew her hand from his arm. 'Forgive me,' she said with irony.

'Your anxiety is natural,' he allowed graciously. 'As I say, we will talk—later.'

She nodded. She could cheerfully have screamed or hit him or burst into tears, but none of these beguiling possibilities would achieve anything but the short-term release of her emotions. And with Roberto Madariaga, she was pretty sure, she could not afford such indulgences. In fact, she needed to do some long-range planning, and fast, before they could talk and he persuade her into doing whatever it was that he no doubt had already planned.

She took a step back from him. 'I'll leave you to greet your friends,' she said. 'I have one or two things to do . . .'

He was bland. 'If you are going to the house, I'll come with you. I need to get out of these clothes.'

She stared at him. 'I want to go to *my* house!'

His mouth twitched. 'You are not yet a property owner in my country, Señorita Lennox. You mean the house you have appropriated.'

'I didn't appropriate it!' Julia said hotly. 'It was lent me. They said the owner was away and wouldn't mind . . .' She trailed into silence as a horrible possibility presented itself to her.

She found Madariaga was smiling encouragingly. 'That's right,' he agreed softly. 'And now the owner has come come. So I'm afraid that—for the immediate future at least—you will have to share it.'

CHAPTER FOUR

SHE sat on the hard wooden chair staring at him blankly. She had not spoken since he had seized her by the elbow and marched her inside. After the brightness of the outdoors, the single room of the house was as black as an underground pit. Even when her eyes got used to it, she could not make out the expression on his face, just the hard features and the glitter of the eyes that seemed to her to be utterly ruthless.

He said, sounding amused, 'Have you gone into shock at the prospect of sharing my living quarters?'

Julia's throat felt as dry as the dust-coated track outside. She swallowed, the sound deafening in the silence, and said baldly, 'Yes.'

He laughed softly, tossing his jacket away from him so that it landed precariously on the corner of the bed. Her eyes followed the garment and another fear, new and very specific, presented itself.

'How very unliberated of you,' he mocked gently.

He was unbuttoning his shirt. Julia tensed instinctively. This was ridiculous, she told herself. He was a sophisticated man, if not a particularly civil one. He had shown no signs of being attracted to her and even if he was—well, sensible men did not assault ladies who attracted them. There was no reason for her to freeze like this, fearful of his purposes and even more fearful of not knowing them.

She said as coolly as she could manage, 'I don't see anything particularly unliberated in not wanting to share living space with my gaoler. Which, after all, is what you are.'

She had angered him; even in the shadowed room she

56

could make out that much. The wicked winging brows twitched together.

'I am not your gaoler,' he said between his teeth. The shirt followed his jacket though, being lighter, it fell short of the bed in a crumpled heap on the woven rug. He did not indicate by so much as the flicker of an eye that he noticed. This, thought Julia grimly, was a man who was used to being waited on.

In answer to his remark she said drily, 'You should see it from where I'm sitting.'

He stared at her frowning. 'You feel like a prisoner? Marta has locked you up? The people have starved you, ignored you, maybe?'

'No,' Julia allowed. '*They* have been most kind.'

'Ah.' He sounded amused again, damn him. 'You think I should have been kinder.' He strolled across and looked down at her consideringly. 'Is that really what you want from me, Señorita Lennox? Kindness?'

Julia was stiff with a prickling awareness in her nerve endings which she was almost sure communicated itself to him. And pleased him. She forced herself to ignore it, meeting his eyes limpidly.

'No,' she agreed softly.

'I thought not.' He did not touch her. The way he looked at her he had no need to touch her. Julia felt as if he had removed her clothes and thoroughly acquainted himself with her body in that one comprehensive look. It took every grain of courage she possessed not to quail, look away, retreat in embarrassment.

But she was an independent lady and she had her self-respect to think of. She would never be able to face herself in the mirror again if she let this callous, laughing pirate get the better of her.

So she leaned back slightly, tipping her head to keep their eyes locked and assumed her most melting expression.

'What I really want from you, Don Roberto——' she

paused and gave him a half smile, 'is my freedom.'

She had underrated him. Not a muscle moved in the carved face. The silvery eyes stayed watchful, unflickering.

'I thought it would be something like that.'

Then he did touch her, an insultingly brief flick of the backs of his fingers against her check. She jumped as if he had burned her, and he laughed harshly.

'I think you want—or at least are in need of—a great deal more than your freedom, Señorita Lennox. To my regret, I do not have the leisure to attend to it.'

Julia flinched at the cool, faintly contemptuous tone. How could Angelina say that he was a man of much passion? He sounded as if he had never had an honest feeling in his life. And as for what he felt for her—well, that was fairly basic, as that stripping glance had made perfectly clear. If she were available, he was perfectly willing to make use of her body temporarily. But he neither liked nor respected her.

The realisation that this man whom she was rapidly coming to identify as her worst enemy neither liked nor respected her filled Julia with desolation, but she refused to betray it to him.

'Do you mean you're going away again?'

A flash of white teeth in an unamused smile. 'No, I do not mean that. I shall be staying here. And you, my little prisoner, will also stay here. But I have not come for a vacation—or for the opportunity of forcing my dastardly attentions upon you, whatever you may fear. I shall be very busy.'

Julia wondered what on earth an international lawyer could find to make him busy in a small village like this, and came to the conclusion that she did not want to know.

'Then of course I must move out of your house,' she said politely. 'You will not want to be disturbed if you're working.'

His mouth twisted wryly. 'You think you will disturb me less if you move out?' When she did not answer—because she did not understand him—he sighed impatiently. 'Unless you are going to camp in the caves there is nowhere else. And mountain nights are very cold.' The dark face took on a mocking expression. 'If you want me to be kind to you, Señorita Lennox, you will allow that it is up to me to see you do not get frostbite in the night.'

She said with very creditable calmness, 'You are all consideration Don Roberto. What do you suggest?'

'I suggest nothing. I am telling you.' Suddenly he sounded very weary. 'Valetta is worried, but at the moment he is not agreeing to anything. Therefore you, my charming bargaining counter, will stay here safe and undetected. You will do whatever you have been doing with your days up to now, and in addition you will keep this house clean and aired; you will wash my clothes, cook my food and run any errands I ask. Is that clear?'

Julia's mouth felt paralysed. 'Perfectly. But it seems rather one-sided. What do I get in return?' she retaliated, sounding, to her own ears, amazingly self-possessed.

The glittering eyes mocked her. 'You get a protector,' he told her in a soft voice that sent shivers of apprehension down her spine.

She raised her eyebrows. 'A protector? To protect me from what?'

'From snakebite,' Roberto told her outrageously and when she gasped, went on with unashamed blandness, 'and landslides and the attentions of the local youths. And, of course,' he added mischievously, 'frostbite.'

Unwillingly Julia's eyes were drawn across the room to the only bed the house possessed which she had hitherto occupied alone.

She said flatly, 'I am not going to sleep with you.'

'You think not?' Roberto's voice was full of wicked laughter. In the darkness she felt her colour rise, but she said steadily,

'Or share a bed with you.'

He said quite calmly, 'I assure you, you are wrong.' He advanced and she sprang out of the chair, nervous as a cat. 'Thank you,' he said politely and, reaching behind her chair, opened the cupboard in front of which she had been sitting, 'my clean shirts are all in here. Perhaps when you have laundered that one—' he indicated the shirt on the floor behind him, 'you will add it to the pile. I think you will find it self-evident which are my country and which my city shirts.'

And he shrugged himself into the clean garment under her furious eyes and strolled out of the house, buttoning it as he went.

When he had gone Julia wandered round the room, hardly knowing what she was doing. Her thoughts were in a turmoil. She felt shivery and clasped her arms across herself to still the erratic tremors that seemed to be shaking her, even though she was not cold.

She tried to marshal her thoughts. This was what she was trained to do, after all: to identify problems and find solutions to them. A soundless laugh shook her. How do you find solutions to unpredictable, shameless pirates like Don Roberto Madariaga? Reproaches amused him and opposition left him unmoved. He would do what he wanted to do and that was all there was to it. It did not matter to him if she resisted him. Julia had the distinct impression that, whether she fell purring into his arms or dug her heels in and screamed defiance, Don Roberto was quite indifferent. The only thing that mattered to him was that, in the end, she did what he wanted; and he did not think that was really in doubt. What she felt about it—what it might cost her—was none of his concern.

She rubbed her arms with her hands. She had not felt so vulnerable, so alone and threatened, for years. Or so unable to cope.

Sit down, she told herself. Sit down and take ten deep

breaths and then analyse the problem from the start.

The breathing exercises calmed her, as they always did. Slowly the shivering stopped. I'm being too dramatic about this, she told herself. I'm allowing that man to panic me and so I'm not thinking clearly. There has to be a rational solution.

First, they're clearly not going to hurt me. They wouldn't have welcomed me into the village as a guest, in the way that they have done, if they were going to torture me or murder me. Anyway, there'd be no point. I'm only worth something to them as long as I'm alive and available for exchange.

Second, they've convinced themselves that their precious Don Roberto has fallen for me so, though they won't hurt me, they won't protect me from him. If I were to try and get away from him the villagers like Angelina would think it was a lovers' quarrel and not want to get involved.

She smiled wryly to herself. In similar circumstances she would not want to get involved either. In engineering such a position Don Roberto, she suspected, had been diabolically clever. He had made himself her gaoler indeed, just as she had accused him.

So—what does Don Roberto intend to do with me, knowing I have nowhere to run to? thought Julia.

And that was the question to which she could not find an answer, no matter how diligently she analysed and deduced. Sometimes she thought his implied threats were no more than a game for his private amusement, a tilt against the independent career woman that he so plainly did not like. Sometimes there was something in those cold eyes that made her feel that he really meant to have her.

No, she thought to herself, so that was not going to happen. She had lived free of sexual commitment since that last day in Hugh's arms. She had wanted nobody and she had not allowed herself to succumb to the persuasions of anyone who wanted her, and Roberto Madariaga was not going to overturn that careful equilibrium. For some obscure reason—no reason at all, just one of her powerful presentiments—Julia was certain that if she ever went into Roberto's arms she would not emerge unscathed. And she knew that pain; she was not going to invite it again.

Do I stay here, then, and let him circle round me like a prowling tiger until I'm so tense I either break into hysteria or give in? she thought. The picture was not a pleasant one. Julia had kept her head in many commercial crises and natural disasters, but she was sure that Roberto Madariaga would test her composure to breaking point. She shuddered as she imagined the scene.

She looked out of the window. The street was empty.

There was only one thing for it. Before Madariaga returned, before he had the chance to subject her to his devilish teasing or, worse, his devilish seduction, she must go. At once.

It proved almost impossible to leave the village. There were too many people, more than she had ever seen, milling about the single street. Most of the faces were unfamiliar to her as hers clearly was to them. She found herself stared at unashamedly. They did not look hostile, but they did look suspicious. She abandoned her plan of slipping away and walking down the hillside to the main road.

Instead she went upwards. She had visited the high fields often enough to know they were criss-crossed with goat and llama trails. One of those, surely, would lead her out of this impossible situation. She strolled casually, as if she were taking a walk for exercise and no other purpose, praying that she would not be noticed. For a while it seemed that she had been successful.

After two hours of walking on baked earth and uneven stones, Julia began to wonder whether her desperate flight was not the silliest thing she had ever done. The burning heat struck up through the thin moccasins that Marta had lent her. The shoes were not tough enough for the climb and they were beginning to sag and flex. More than once they sent her lurching sideways.

In the end it was almost a relief when she heard her name called. She had no further energy to run, even if there had been anywhere to run to. She turned, shaking the sweat-dampened hair out of her eyes, like an exhausted animal at bay.

It was, inevitably she felt, Roberto. He looked cooler than she would have believed possible and very fit, as if he could have carried on that punishing climb for ever. In comparison with her own distressed state, it was almost an insult.

She stood quite still, her breasts heaving with the effort of breathing the thin dry air, and glared at him. He stopped a few paces away from her and looked up quizzically.

'You know,' said Roberto Madariaga in a thoughtful voice, 'you are really extremely resourceful. I congratulate you, Señorita Lennox.'

She pushed her hair back with a hand that shook slightly. 'Thank you,' she said between her teeth.

He smiled at her. 'Not a lot of forethought, of course. But resourceful nevertheless. And brave.' He strolled the rest of the way up the slope towards her, as surefooted on the pebble-strewn ground as if it were a Manhattan sidewalk. Julia tensed uncontrollably. 'In spite of myself, I find things in you to admire, Señorita Lennox.'

His tone was mocking. Julia knew that he meant the exact reverse.

'Don't laugh at me,' she said in a suffocated voice.

'Then don't be ridiculous!' His voice sharpened. 'Do you realise you could kill yourself, scrambling over this sort of terrain? Without even the right equipment.' He pointed scathingly to the battered moccasins. 'And what

were you going to do when night fell? Freeze? And all for
what, on a path that goes nowhere except towards the
summit! Did you think you would escape over the
mountains to freedom like some heroine out of a
melodrama?'

Julia bit her lip. That was, she supposed, exactly what
she had thought.

'You must have expected me to do *something*,' she said
wearily.

'Perhaps I did,' he acknowledged, with a private smile.
'But not this.'

'What, then?' She was so tired her head was spinning
but she sensed obscurely that, if she could discover what
he thought of her, what he expected her to do, she would
be better armed for the future.

He shrugged. 'Oh, something guileful and feminine.'

Before she could answer, he took her arm firmly,
turning her towards the animal track in the scrubbed
earth. She jumped under the hard grip of his fingers and
was instantly assailed by a great tide of weakness,
washing through her like the sea. She swayed.

'You are exhausted.' He was frowning. She supposed
he was disgusted by her feeble reactions.

She shook herself free of him, fighting back tiredness
that was like a blanket. 'A spot of hard walking never
hurt anyone,' she said evenly. 'Unlike terrorists.'

For a moment she almost thought he flinched.
Certainly his face darkened and a muscle began to twitch
in his cheek. She watched it, trying to concentrate on
that, on anything, rather than the surge of previously
suppressed fear that she could feel beginning to build up
inside her.

'I think you know that we are not terrorists,' he said.
'Otherwise you would not dare to say such a thing to me.'

She straightened her shoulders and looked him in the
eye. 'Don't you like the truth, Don Roberto?' she
challenged, sinking her fear in mockery.

There was a pause, then he said, 'When you know the truth, I might be prepared to debate the matter with you. But you are ignorant, a foreigner, you know nothing of this country or of myself.'

She said very softly, 'I know you kidnapped me.'

The silence was electric. His eyes bored into hers, hot and fierce. She did not give him the satisfaction of seeing her apprehension, though it took an enormous effort of will. She met his eyes unflinchingly.

He said harshly, shockingly, 'Then don't forget it,' and pulled her hard towards him.

She could feel his heart racing and shrank. Not all her self-control, not all her determined courage, could have prevented her. His mouth twisted.

'We will return to the village—now. If you resist, I will carry you, if necessary. If you try to run away, I shall tie you up.' His voice was flat and without emotion. 'You would be wiser not to put me to that trouble.'

They did not speak during the dreadful descent. Julia stumbled so often that he had to help her, but he did so grimly, with hands that were impersonal and yet almost cruel. A couple of times she caught her breath in a quickly suppressed exclamation of pain, but all it earned her was a brief, unsmiling look.

In the village, Angelina came rushing towards them, though it was already dark, as if she had been waiting. She sounded anxious. Roberto only answered her queries curtly, though, and Angelina stepped back at once, releasing Julia to his possessive arm. His hand clamped hard into Julia's waist so that she flinched and had to bite back an exclamation of pain.

'I will see you later, Angelina. The *señorita* needs to rest after her little adventure, so she will not be eating with you tonight,' he announced before leading Julia off, with every appearance of solicitude, to his house.

Inside somebody had already lit the oil lamp. It made the interior look warm and oddly homelike. Julia felt unexpected tears prick her eyes and turned her head away before he should see them.

Roberto, however, was not looking at her. He was closing both halves of the door. Julia watched him with misgiving. He went to the window and drew the shutters closed across that as well. The silence tautened her nerves unbearably.

To break it she said in a high, affected voice which she barely recognised as her own, 'Are you going to beat me for running away? Don't you want the village to see?'

He faced her. 'You would deserve it if I did. How could you be so thoughtless? Don't you realise you could have broken a leg scrambling up the mountain like that? Possibly even your neck!'

'Don't you reckon much to your chances of negotiating if you've only got a corpse to bargain with?' Julia mocked him.

She thought for a moment she had made him angry, but he only said blandly, 'None at all.'

'So what are you going to do with me?' she demanded.

'Well, obviously, keep you alive,' said Roberto, his mouth quirking. 'By hook or by crook.'

She said, 'I meant—now.'

'Ah, now.' He was thoughtful. 'I told Angelina that you should rest, and I think perhaps I was right.'

He advanced towards her. Refusing to give ground, Julia raised her chin and looked him straight in the eye.

'If you lay a hand on me, I shall scream so loud they'll hear me in the next valley!'

To her chagrin Roberto only looked amused. 'That will enhance my reputation enormously.'

She said on a note of courteous enquiry, 'Reputation for violence?'

He laughed out loud at that. 'You really are determined to enrage me, aren't you?'

There was nothing Julia dreaded more, but she was not

going to admit that. She said, 'I just want to get the position clear.'

Roberto smiled. 'But it is quite clear. You are my— hostage. Your wellbeing is my responsibility. You resent this, but you cannot change it.'

'My wellbeing?' she echoed in disdain.

'Your physical safety, comfort and, I hope, pleasure,' he explained, looking innocent.

Julia gasped and sat down hard on the nearest object, which happened to be the corner of the built-in bed. He watched her with interest.

'You are feeling tired? You perhaps expended more effort on your walk than you bargained for?' he asked with what Julia knew was spurious solicitude.

She glared at him. 'I am not in the least tired——'

'Good,' he interrupted, and was across the room in a single stride. The words died in her throat as he took her shoulders between his hands and lifted her slowly to her feet. He subjected her to a searching look which she withstood with rather less than the calm she would have liked. He appeared faintly puzzled.

'Why are you so frightened? You must realise that if I have not murdered you by now I am probably not going to,' Roberto said wryly.

Her throat closed, but she managed to say, 'I'm not in the least frightened.'

He lifted her hand and laid it against his chest where they could both feel the little tremors that were shuddering through her fingers. He raised one eyebrow. 'No?'

Her eyes fell and she bit her lip. He took her chin between thumb and forefinger quite gently.

'Then why are you shaking? Do you really think I would hurt you?'

She swallowed. 'I don't know.'

Roberto looked sardonic. 'Would it help if I told you that rape has never been one of my favourite pastimes?'

Julia flushed and found, to her surprise and horror, that it did not help at all. Rape was not what she feared from Roberto Madariaga; it was all more complicated than that.

He misinterpreted her silence. 'I admit you've made me very angry. Until I met you I'd always regarded myself as a peaceable man,' he said meditatively. 'But in the last few days I have twice come closer to striking a woman than I would ever have believed possible.'

Julia was anxious and uncertain; he muddled her and intimidated her and had a strange effect on her pulses. But she was not willing to let this pass.

'Are you saying that it's my fault you bully me?' she demanded in an incredulous tone.

To her surprise he flushed. His hands fell away and he half turned so she was looking only at the firm profile.

'You bring out the worst in me,' he admitted ruefully. 'I don't know whether it's your fault or mine.'

Julia watched him. The alarm was draining out of her, leaving her tired and oddly dispirited.

'Don't you?' she asked wearily.

He shrugged. 'Well, yes, I suppose I do. We're not children, you and I. I guess we both know.'

Julia did not understand him, so she said nothing.

'Only the timing is damnable,' said Roberto, almost to himself.

This time she said it. 'I don't understand.'

He sent her a quick look. 'Don't you? Well, take it from me, it couldn't be worse. The country is in a ferment, it could blow up at any moment.' He looked rueful. 'To be honest I don't know that it hasn't already. None of the radio stations has been broadcasting for twenty-four hours. Or none except the Army station, and all that has been playing is recorded music.'

Julia said, catching her breath, 'You mean there's going to be a revolution?'

'Almost certainly.' He pushed a hand through his hair

distractedly. 'And very soon, if not now, even as we speak.'

She gave a little shiver. 'How terrible!'

Roberto was wry. 'Not so terrible for us. We've virtually been living in a revolution for years. Now is the chance to settle things once and for all and get some orderly government back into my poor country.'

He did not, thought Julia, bewildered, sound like an impassioned revolutionary. In fact he sounded immen—sely weary.

She said, 'How will you be involved? Will you,' she swallowed, 'fight?'

He spun round to face her, the sleet-cold eyes glinting with mockery.

'What do you mean by fighting, Señorita Lennox? You fight your competitors, don't you? With better deals and extra-contractual perks and the slush fund?'

Julia remembered President Valetta's proposition that Technica syphon off some of the project's funds into a Swiss bank account in his private name. She laughed, shaking her head.

'You don't want to believe everything you read in the papers.'

'No?' Roberto looked at her curiously. 'Are you telling me you don't use bribery when it proves necessary, Señorita Lennox?' His voice became menacingly soft, with a sudden change of mood that brought all the hairs on the back of Julia's neck up in chilling apprehension. 'You mean that if I, for example, were in a position to award you this dam contract you would not try to persuade me to do so?'

Julia met his eyes squarely. 'Well, of course I would. It's a good project and your country needs it. Technica isn't the only company that thinks so. But I wouldn't be mobilising any imaginary slush fund to do so.'

He smiled, not pleasantly. 'You mean your persuasion would take other forms?' And as she continued to stare at him he went on, 'Well, that's shrewd enough.'

Julia's mouth was dry. She said with an effort, 'I don't know what you're talking about.'

'Oh, I think you do, my dear. You're a very intelligent lady.'

She shook her head.

Roberto said harshly, 'Then let me make myself plain: as has been obvious to you from the start, I want you. That, as you have realised, puts a weapon in your hands. But God help you if you try to use it!'

Julia was very white, but she said with reasonable calm, 'You talk as if I'm a combatant in this revolution of yours. I assure you I'm not.'

'No,' he agreed. The harshness was gone from his voice. 'No, you're safe here, and this is where you'll stay.'

'*Here*?' Julia's eyes went back to the bed as if drawn by a magnet.

Roberto's mouth twisted. 'I said safe,' he reminded her. 'I shan't touch you. Quite apart from the fact that I find rape highly unamusing, I shall be very busy. You can make yourself useful on the domestic front, but I can assure you that those are all the services I shall be requiring from you.'

He picked up a safari jacket from the back of the chair and swung it over his shoulder. At the door he looked back.

'Unless, of course,' he said softly, 'you decide you want it otherwise.'

And went out.

CHAPTER FIVE

JULIA did not see him again that night, though she sat up till her eyelids were drooping and her every third breath was a yawn. In the end she knew she could not keep awake any longer, so she crawled under the sunburst cover without removing any but her outer garments.

When she finally opened her eyes in the morning it was still dark, but there were clear sounds of activity outside. She struggled round on to one elbow to peer at her watch but it had stopped. In the movement, though, she caught sight of the shutters, still firmly barred against the outside world, and realised why it was dark.

Of Roberto there was no sign. Julia had tossed and turned in her sleep so that the bedclothes were in considerable disarray, but there was only one imprint of a head on the pillow. So he had not shared the bed with her last night.

She looked round the room. There was nowhere else he could comfortably have slept—the chair was hard and uncushioned; the floor was stone. So he must have slept elsewhere, she reasoned with an odd little fall of the heart. At some point he must have returned, though, for the jacket he had taken with him was hanging on the back of a chair by the table and a neat pile of clothes, which she had little trouble identifying as those he had worn yesterday, was placed on the seat. Julia supposed, resentfully, that he would expect her to wash them.

She pushed the bedclothes away and scrambled up. She herself had nothing to wear except the clothes that Marta had lent her. This, irrationally, added to her annoyance. The shirt was stiff with dust and to her fastidious nose smelled faintly of stale sweat. It was not really surprising, she thought, considering her efforts of yesterday, but it made the garment unthinkable to put on.

Julia cast it away with an exclamation of annoyance and eyed the chest speculatively. Roberto had said he kept clean clothes there. Perhaps it would give forth a fresh blouse that had been left by a lady visitor. Or, failing that, one of his own light cotton shirts. It would be ludicrously too big, of course, but Marta had lent her a leather belt and she could cinch it in at the waist easily enough. Anything would be preferable to Marta's shirt until she had washed it.

She took a step towards the chest and made a discovery. She could barely walk.

She gasped and sat down very suddenly on the edge of the bed rubbing the calf of her right leg. It felt as if it was on fire. She stretched it cautiously in front of her and winced almost at once. The muscle virtually refused to stretch, and it was agony to point her toe. Yesterday's scramble down the mountain had cost her more than she thought.

She sat very still for a moment, getting her breath back. At least she need not move too much here. She thought with sudden clarity of what it would have been like awaking in her stony shelter with muscles like this. She would never have got any further, she realised. Her plans for walking back to Alto Rio had been pure fantasy. She had been lucky, in a way, that Madariaga had found her; he had identified the dangers a lot more scientifically than she had done.

She supposed, Julia thought drily, she owed him a debt of gratitude. If he had not discovered her she would have been stuck halfway down the mountainside unable to move for who knew how long? And the nights, as he had reminded her, were cold. She resolved to tell him she was grateful: it was only fair, no matter how much she detested the odious, superior beast.

The thought of how much she owed him confirmed Julia in her intention to filch one of his shirts. If she had to be grateful to him, it would be on grounds of her own choosing!

Very carefully she made her way across to the chest. Though it hurt, she could walk if she swung her legs from the hip and put her feet down flat. It was not locked. It was full of books and papers and maps with a small machine that at first she thought was a portable music centre. Then, looking at its dials and buttons, she realised what it was: a two-way radio.

Julia felt her heart contract with trepidation. She had managed to forget it in her deep dreams last night, and in her preoccupation this morning, but this was no game with just herself and Roberto Madariaga circling round each other like duellists. This was real and important, and people would probably die. She, Julia Lennox, was completely irrelevant to the course of the struggle and, probably, to Roberto Madariaga. The best thing she could do would be to keep quiet, keep out of the way and hope to be reunited with her colleagues in the course of time.

She abstracted a shirt at random and pulled it on, shaking her dark hair out over the collar. Roberto must have been speaking the truth when he said she was a nuisance, she realised bleakly.

A voice spoke behind her. 'Very nice.'

She turned—carefully, because of the pain of her strained muscles—and saw the object of her thoughts standing in the half open doorway. Behind him it was full daylight.

She raised her brows. 'Nice?'

The long mouth curled into a smile. She could not read his eyes.

'My shirt has seldom appeared so decorative. I suppose you are suffering badly from the loss of your wardrobe. What happened to that fetching nonsense you were wearing in the nightclub?'

Julia said, 'I haven't the faintest idea. Marta provided me with the jeans,' she nodded in the direction of the chair on which she had left her own clothes last night, 'so I imagine she has it somewhere.' She smiled wryly. 'In the circumstances, I think she has the worst of the bargain.'

Roberto laughed. 'You are very philosophical. You're probably right. But I shall see you get the dress back.'

Julia shrugged. 'Don't bother—it was never a favourite and I should think it's beyond repair by now.'

'It was torn?' Suddenly he was frowning blackly. 'How?'

She was surprised. 'On various extruding mechanical parts in the jeep, mainly. Where it acquired several gouts of oil, as well. I suspect it's just about ready to be cut up for dusters.'

This time he was puzzled, though the frown was no less dire. 'Dusters?'

Julia grinned at him. 'An old Scottish custom. In my aunt's house, where I was brought up, clothes were worn until they were threadbare and were then cut up into neat squares with which to clean the windows and polish the furniture. Dusters.'

'Good God!' He sounded completely blank. 'And you did this? This washing windows and—and everything? You?'

'Certainly,' she said coolly. 'You need have no fear that you're leaving your housekeeping in the hands of an amateur. If you intend to hold by your original plan, that is?' and she raised an enquiring eyebrow at him.

'I am more than ever convinced of the rightness of it,' he said smoothly, with a long considering look at her still bare legs. He raised his eyes to hers and there was a distinct challenge in them to which Julia, conscious that she could move neither fast nor gracefully, refused to respond. 'I just came back to tell you that I am going over to the next village with Pepe, so I will not be back until this evening. And to warn you that if you try to run away again, I shall tie you to a chair for the rest of the time you are with us. So this is your last chance.'

Julia swallowed. He did not sound menacing; he sounded amused. But nevertheless, she knew he was serious. In his position, so would she have been. An irrelevance she might be, but her escape could cause him loss of credibility with his comrades, if nothing worse.

She nodded slowly.

Roberto's eyes narrowed. 'No more attempts to bolt?'

Her mouth moved in a smile which he must have seen was forced. 'No. I realise what dangers I was running yesterday. I must have been a little mad, I think. I don't know the country and, I have now discovered, I'm not nearly fit enough.'

He took this news without surprise. 'Stiff, are you?' he asked unsympathetically. 'Let it be a lesson to you. You'll loosen up as you start to move about. If you don't, ask Angelina for some of her ointment. It smells disgusting, but the villagers swear by it.'

'Thank you,' said Julia drily. 'I'll try my best to do without the ointment.'

Roberto laughed. 'It's excellent,' he assured her. 'It even keeps the mosquitoes away.'

'You've tried it yourself?' she asked suspiciously.

'Well, no, but I've been within hailing distance of people who have,' he told her solemnly.

She groaned. 'Excellent. I suppose it also keeps people away?'

She expected him to laugh again, but he did not. Instead, inexplicably, his face darkened. His eyes avoided hers.

'That might not be such a bad thing,' he said after a pause.

Julia's eyebrows twitched together in a quick frown. 'I don't understand.'

Roberto seemed to hesitate. 'No, I dare say you don't. It's not easy to explain.' He fell silent, looking worried.

She felt incomprehensibly moved. Almost she went to him, reached out in a gesture of some sort of comfort, but she suppressed the instinct firmly. He did not want comfort from her. He would be astounded, probably profoundly embarrassed, if she offered it. And she had no business in wanting to comfort him either. Was he not her enemy?

So she said in a cool little voice, 'Try.'

He gave her a quick look, noting the coolness. He thrust his hands into his pockets, half-turning away from her.

'You must understand what is going on here. This country has been in a ferment for years, and there are factions everywhere. For there to be some sort of coherent action we all have to work together.' He paused. 'Some of the men I have to work with, therefore, are not necessarily the colleagues I would choose. Do I make myself clear?'

Julia thought of the strange men she had seen in the village the night before and the way some of them had stared at her. She shivered.

'I can see you do.' Roberto's voice was dry.

Julia's mouth was dry. That familiar sensation of cold fear began to lick round her nerves again. She said tightly, 'I thought you said you were not terrorists.'

To her surprise he flushed darkly, his lips twisting.

'Yes, I like to keep my hands clean, don't I,' he said with a trace of bitterness.

'You mean it's not true?'

Oh God, she was beginning to shake again, as the horror of her imaginings re-emerged.

'It's true as far as it goes. Of myself and my—companions.' He suddenly thrust a hand through his hair as if he were furious or desperately bewildered. 'But I can't answer for some of the others, my so-called allies. I can't answer for them, but I need them.'

'And you think they'd hurt me?' Julia asked slowly.

His look was ironic. 'I think they'd do to you whatever they thought they'd enjoy,' he said with deliberate brutality, and, when she gasped, went on, 'which is why I'd feel happier if you kept out of their way.'

Julia swallowed. 'Then why did you bring me here?' she said in little more than a whisper. She tried to disguise her fear but she did not make much of a fist of it, she knew. It was palpable in her white face and shaky tones.

He shrugged. 'A miscalculation on my part.'

'*Miscalculation*?' Her voice rose in outrage.

'I freely admit it. If I had realised how close the revolution was, then I would have taken you to my mother, no matter what.'

She stared at him, utterly silenced. He met her look, half grim, half rueful.

'Don't look like that. Did you think I was too inhuman to have a mother?' She shook her head helplessly and the rueful expression died away. 'It would be no great surprise if you did. It's the view my mother seems to hold, anyway.'

'Does your mother know about me?' asked Julia slowly.

Roberto shrugged. 'I wouldn't be surprised,' he said enigmatically. 'She seems to know most things—it's her speciality. But if you're asking me whether I've told her anything about you, the answer is no.'

Again there was that odd note of bitterness under the air of indifference. Julia looked at him, puzzled.

He went on, 'But she would have given you house room. She would have felt I had let the family down—again—and it was up to her to make reparation. And, God help us both, I didn't want that, so I brought you here.' He shut his eyes briefly. 'And I'm going to have the devil's own job keeping you safe. I suppose it's no more

than I deserve, but you——' He drew a breath before
continuing more moderately, 'I can't help seeing that it's
hard luck on you. None of this is your fault, after all.'

There was a tense little silence. Julia watched him in
bewilderment. She could see that he was full of anger and
other emotions which she did not know him well enough
to guess at. In spite of that, she found to her surprise and
faint alarm that the urge to comfort him continued
unabated.

She said calmly, 'That may be so, but I'm here now.
You must tell me what I have to do.' He gave her an
incredulous look which she met with a faint smile. 'To
ensure my safety and your peace of mind,' she explained,
'since they appear to be inextricably bound up together.'

'Yes, they do, don't they?' Roberto agreed slowly, not
taking his eyes from her. His eyes had narrowed, as if he
was contemplating some perspective which he had not
previously seen and which did not altogether delight
him.

Julia said, 'Well?'

He seemed to give himself a little shake.

'Your own common sense will be your best guide.' His
return to briskness seemed to cost him an effort. 'Stay out
of sight as much as you can. If you have to go out, stay
close to Angelina.'

Her mouth stretched in a pitiful attempt at a smile.
'And don't talk to strangers?' she suggested, trying to
laugh.

'Exactly.' He came towards her and looked down into
her face for a moment, his expression sober. 'Don't look
so alarmed. Whatever I can do to keep you out of harm,
shall be done.'

It sounded like a vow, and Julia was shaken by it,
moved in spite of herself. Reluctantly, she found herself
returning his regard.

'Trust me,' he said, under his breath.

She found that she did, though all her intelligence and

instincts warred against it. She was not, however, so
unguarded as to admit it.

'I will follow your advice,' she said, not answering.

There was a pause, then he said drily, 'That's
something, I suppose.'

She raised cool eyebrows. 'Everything, surely?'

'Everything?'

'Everything that you want from me,' she elaborated.
'Obedience, I mean.'

His face stilled as a guarded look entered his eyes.

'I do not think either of us would find it very
satisfactory if I told you everything I wanted from you,'
he said at last. 'Not for the moment, anyway. We can
speak of it another time. In the meantime, I am late and
will have to go.' Still, in spite of his words, he hesitated,
almost as if he were expecting a gesture of farewell, a
touch or a kiss.

Julia stood rigid, bewildered and torn. She could not
kiss him goodbye, she did not want to. She was not even
entirely sure that he wanted her to. And yet . . .

He turned away. 'I shall be back this evening,' he said,
not looking at her. 'Be careful.' And he was gone.

Julia was left on her own, stiff and aching, inwardly as
well as out. For a moment it had seemed as if he was
asking her for something and she had felt unwilling to
withhold it, yet terrified to surrender it. She gave herself
a shake. This was foolish. What she needed was activity.
She would do the laundry.

She sought Angelina's advice. The older woman was
helpfulness itself, though a little amused. She did not
mention Roberto, but this omission had so much the
appearance of deliberate tact that Julia was embarrassed
by it and went quite pink. Angelina, hugely pleased, lent
her soap and showed her the part of the stream they used
first to wash and then to rinse their clothes. Afterwards,
she instructed, Julia should lay things across the
surrounding low bushes. In the midday sun, they would

dry in a matter of hours, even the heavy denim.

Julia followed instructions to the letter. It was with a sense of fulfilment that, she realised, she had not felt since she had last seen a watercourse that she had built begin slowly to fill with water, that she returned to the site to discover everything clean, dry and smelling sweetly of the herbal bush on which it had dried. She folded the clothes carefully and took them back to the house, passing a dried-out field of corn as she went.

Marta was standing there, looking at it sadly. There were two men working in the fields, standing and bending amid the plants which were not much higher than tufts.

'What is the growing season here?' asked Julia, casting a professional eye over the plants. By their height they should not be very mature but already they were turning the dry straw colour that signified either the end of the growing season or a severe lack of water.

Marta sighed. 'These should be ready for harvesting. But,' she made a despairing gesture, 'they are as you see.'

Julia hunkered down on her haunches and let the earth run through her fingers. It was stony, powdery. Without her kit she had no way of telling what its mineral properties were but it did not look like a poor soil lacking in nutrients.

She asked with a nod to the field, 'Have you always grown maize?'

'As long as I can remember. Most of our food is made from maize flour.'

'And you can grow enough to feed the village?'

Marta's eyes were shadowed. 'We used to be able to. Now—no. Even though so many have moved out of the village.'

Julia looked down at the earth as if it absorbed her. 'You mean people like Roberto?' she asked casually.

Marta laughed. 'Oh, Don Roberto never lived here, Señorita Lennox.'

'No?' Julia stood up, flaking earth carefully through her fingers. She managed to sound quite preoccupied. 'Yet it's his house that I'm living in?'

'But of course.' Marta did not try to disguise her surprise. 'His family own all the land round here, most of the houses too.'

Julia thought of the radio, the store of clean clothes in the house, and raised her eyebrows. Seeing it, Marta shrugged.

'The house used to be lived in by a woman who was his nurse for many years. When she died he decided to use it as a base, a headquarters that nobody knew about. That was several years ago. Now, of course, many people know about it. Perhaps too many.'

'Too many?' Julia's head went up. There was something in Marta's tone that disturbed her. 'Do you mean that somebody might betray him? That he's in danger?'

Marta looked at her levelly. 'These are dangerous times for us all, *señorita*.'

Julia was reminded of the night she had been kidnapped, how cool Marta had seemed then. She seemed equally unmoved now. Julia shivered. Although the girl was friendly enough, there was little sign that in an emergency she would have any compunction at all in dispatching their hostage.

She looked down at the crumbs of earth in her hand. 'I'm not a danger to any of you, Marta,' she said abruptly.

Again the girl shrugged, not answering.

'I'm not,' Julia insisted. 'I wouldn't know how to be. I know nothing about your politics.'

Marta looked faintly scornful. But all she said, in the same even tone, was, 'It is not essential to know a great deal to constitute a danger to other people, *señorita*.'

Julia shook her head, uncomprehending. 'But how?'

'I do not know,' Marta said fairmindedly. 'I cannot tell. But it makes me uneasy this state of emergency in the capital, all these people seeking out Don Roberto, when he ought to be in the city far away from us. It is all happening too soon, too hurriedly. The government have been put on their guard.'

'And it's my fault?' Julia's eyes darkened. 'How can you say that? It's not fair!'

'It may not be fair,' Marta was relentless, 'but it has all happened since you came to us.' She put her hands on her hips, her feet apart and regarded Julia dispassionately. 'The truth is that ever since Don Roberto found we had taken you instead of the man, he has been ignoring the plans, taking risks, acting on impulse.' She sighed deeply. 'Breaching security. Some of our allies are beginning to say that maybe he is not reliable.'

'And that's my fault?' cried Julia, stung.

Marta was sarcastic. 'Can you honestly say that it is not? Do you think Don Roberto would have moved up into the mountains a month early to make sure your male colleague came to no harm at our hands?'

Julia was very pale. 'Do you hate me?'

'I? No!' The girl sounded genuinely startled. 'I believe that Don Roberto knows what he is doing and would not be swayed by a pretty face. But I cannot hide from myself the fact that he is not as secure as he might have been—as he should have been—if you had not come along.'

Julia swallowed. 'What can I do?' she asked in a low voice.

Marta looked down at the baked earth. 'You were talking about the crops as if you know something about them. Concentrate on that.'

'Willingly.' Julia nodded but was faintly puzzled. 'But how will that help?'

Marta gave her a straight look. 'It will suggest that Don Roberto keeps you here to help the village smallholders, not to warm his bed alone,' she said crisply.

Julia drew a sharp breath and stepped back as if she had been struck. There was no malice in Marta's voice, though. She did not seem to resent the relationship she assumed, any more than she doubted its existence. Her only concern—her whole demeanour made it plain—was Roberto's credibility.

But Julia could not take it so coolly. She supposed that if she had thought about it she would have realised that the village must have believed they were lovers. Angelina, with her sentimental sighings, certainly did. But Julia had been so bound up in her own thoughts and fears she had not spared speculation on what anybody else might think. Now the revelation that she was assumed to be Don Roberto Madariaga's mistress filled her with horror and embarrassment.

She said with difficulty, 'It isn't what you think . . .'

But Marta interrupted her. 'What I think does not matter, *señorita*. It is what the local leaders think that matters. And, I suppose, his family.'

Julia eyes narrowed. 'His family?'

'You really do know nothing!' Marta was faintly impatient. 'The Madariagas are very rich, very powerful—and very unhappy. Doña Eleanora and Don Felipe have lived apart for many years and the children—Don Roberto's brother and sisters—are difficult and disturbed. Doña Eleanora wants Don Roberto to marry a lady who will make a new family home where they can all go to be put on the rails again.'

Julia said with an effort, 'And what has all that to do with me?'

'Perhaps nothing.' Marta gave her a sideways look, before bending to pick up the bundle of clean laundry Julia had left on a flat stone before she started to look at the maize. 'Only Doña Eleanora says that he accepts this. He knows he must marry. He has promised her that he will do so when the present emergency is over, no matter what happens to the government.'

'So?'

Marta handed her the laundry. 'He has never been a

saint, you understand. But apparently he gave Doña Eleanora an undertaking that he would—regularise—his life.'

Julia shifted the bundle to her hip, as she had seen the women in the village do, and managed an expression of indifferent amusement.

'You know a great deal about this family, señorita.'

Marta gave her an unshadowed smile. 'I should. It was my sister Florita whom he had to regularise,' she said ruefully. 'Neither of them appreciated it at the time. And if it is all for nothing because he has replaced her with you, I don't know who will be the more mad—Doña Eleanora or my sister.'

This frankness utterly silenced Julia.

After a pause, Marta went on, 'So you see, it would be better for all of us if you continue your interest in our crops rather than our gallant leader.'

'Yes, I can see that,' Julia said with difficulty. 'But he told me—that is, he warned me not to be too visible. Because of the strangers in the village.'

Marta nodded in sober agreement. 'I am inclined to agree with him. On the other hand, if you stay in the high fields you will be out of their sight. They will not leave the village.'

Julia nodded. 'Very well. Will you show me the main water source?'

'With pleasure.' Again Marta gave her that open friendly smile, as if they were ordinary professional colleagues. As if she had not just turned Julia's world upside down again with her talk of the beautiful dancer, Florita, and the rumour that she, Julia Lennox, had replaced her in Don Roberto Madariaga's affections.

They went back to the village together, Julia strained and silent, though Marta continued to talk calmly about the village and its inhabitants. They parted at the door of Roberto's house. Julia's farewell was perfunctory. She could hardly wait to close the door on her companion and be alone. The information that Marta had imparted disturbed her profoundly.

In the dark little room, she put down her pile of laundry carefully. The room was as tidy as she had left it; Roberto had obviously not returned in her absence. Nevertheless, she felt he was still there, an almost tangible presence, touching her nerve-endings into awareness. She shivered.

It was sexual tension, she thought, nothing more or less than the effect of proximity and a reasonably strong attraction. If they had met in New York, or even Alto Rio, neither of them would have been too much affected by it. There would have been too many other people around, the effect would have been neutralised. And there would have been too much else to do. But here—when they were on top of each other, or likely to be for long stretches of time—they were too appallingly close to ignore that attraction or to see it in its proper perspective.

Julia began methodically to tidy the clothes she had washed and put them away in the ancient cupboard. Her hands were shaking very slightly.

She must keep busy, she resolved. If she did not, if she succumbed to this unfamiliar feeling that she only dimly recognised but the villagers seemed to have identified without surprise, immediately, then, she would be radically changed. She would lose a part of herself. She could not afford that; not if she were ever to return to her former life, her career, her peace of mind.

She must keep busy. And she must keep out of his way. Though God knew how, in the enforced intimacy of the little village house, she was going to be able to do that.

It was not, in the end, all that difficult. Roberto returned late that night and other nights, and was away sometimes before it was light in the morning. So when she saw him, Julia was usually muzzy and half asleep. He laughed at her drowsiness, but he did not try to dispel it. Julia began to feel that he was a dream figure, a creature she only encountered in the twilight world between sleep and waking when, uncharacteristically, he seemed almost tender.

That, she was convinced, was the genuine stuff of dreams, some sort of wistful hangover from her sleeping fantasies. She could not imagine Roberto being tender with anyone. Passionate, yes. She was certain, though she did not know why, that, if he were really involved, he would be a passionate lover, impossible to relegate to the shadows with daylight.

It remained a mystery. Did he really hold her in his arms during the hours of darkness? Could he possibly turn back from the doorway to drop a light kiss on her hair before he strode out into the cool morning? It seemed hardly credible.

It was, she told herself sternly, the merest wish-fulfilment. And then she started to worry about why she should wish for such signs of affection from a man who had kidnapped and virtually imprisoned her. Not liking her conclusions, she would then fling herself into the crop investigation project that Marta had suggested, toiling up mountain paths and tracing streams until she was so weary she could barely stand.

It did not banish Roberto's image. Nor did it solve the mystery of where he went during the day. But it did prevent Julia from working herself into hysteria, as she wryly acknowledged to herself.

Her resolution to think as little as possible about the man was not helped by Angelina's comfortable conviction that Don Roberto was hopelessly in love with their guest. She was naturally friendly, it was clear, and she seemed to have taken a fancy to Julia, but it was plain that all the things she was anxious to show her were part of a daily life that she fully expected Julia would share in the future.

'Don Roberto,' she would say, as one quoting an oracle, 'always likes . . .' and off she would go, describing the way that things had to be done for that demanding man.

Eventually Julia felt she could endure it no longer. Suppressing embarrassment, she tried to protest in a moderate tone.

'I'm not going to be here for very long, you know, Angelina,' she said gently one day as she was being instructed in the art of making the local bean soup. 'When Don Roberto hears from the President, he will return me to the capital.'

Angelina waved this away. 'But you will return.'

'I would like to, certainly, but it may not be possible. My work takes up all my time and I have to travel all over the world . . .'

She trailed off into silence as she found Angelina regarding her with faint disdain.

'Don Roberto,' Angelina said firmly, 'comes here regularly. You will not let your work interfere with that.'

'Well, no, of course not, but . . .'

'There you are, then!' Angelina was triumphant. 'When he comes here, you will come.' She turned back to the cooking pot.

'Angelina, will you *listen* to me!' cried Julia in exasperation. 'When I leave here I'm never going to see your Don Roberto again. Do you understand that?'

Angelina looked wise and knowing. 'Who can tell the future?' she answered airily.

'I can,' retorted Julia, not to be gainsaid. 'Look,' she took the ladle out of the older woman's hand and turned her round to face her, holding both her hands, 'you've been very kind to me, all of you, and I'm grateful—really grateful. But that doesn't mean I'm going to become the permanent plaything of your Don Roberto.'

Angelina looked shocked. 'But of course not! A nice girl like you.' She stroked Julia's dark hair affectionately. 'He can behave very badly when he is in a temper, but he would not expect *that*.'

'I don't think he thinks I'm a nice girl at all,' said Julia ruefully, temporarily deflected.

'That would be his temper. Always from a small boy he has exploded when his plans are upset.'

'Oh, that's what it was, was it? I shall take care not to upset his plans again, in that case.' Julia was dry.

'Excellent,' said a cool voice from the doorway behind them.

Julia swung round so fast that she knocked the ladle out of Angelina's hand and it fell to the stone floor with a clatter. In some confusion, she darted after it, aware that her cheeks were pink and hoping that Roberto would either not notice or would ascribe it to her energetic dash for the ladle. From the sardonic look in his eye, she doubted whether her hopes would be realised.

But all he said was, 'I apologise for startling you, but I need to talk to Señorita Lennox.'

Angelina beamed on him. 'But of course.'

Julia said nothing, quietly putting the ladle on the hearth where Angelina could find it easily. Roberto gave her a frowning sideways look.

'Were you busy?'

'No.' She struggled to keep her voice neutral, surprised and alarmed at the great leap of delighted recognition that her heart had taken at the sound of his voice. 'But I was going to the maize fields above the village.'

'Then I will escort you,' he said formally.

He made it sound as if they were taking a promenade in the Bois de Boulogne, Julia thought a little hysterically. She cast a quick look at him under her lashes but, as usual, found his face unreadable. She bent her head in acquiescence and preceded him quietly out of the house. Behind her she could feel the heat of Angelina's benevolent, sentimental gaze, like the rays of a sun lamp on the back of her neck. She blushed again.

Roberto said curiously, 'I seem to have upset you. You are very pink.'

Damn him, thought Julia, but she answered sweetly, 'The heat of the fire. I can see why the people here don't normally cook during the day.'

'Oh, is that what it is?' He sounded mocking but he did not press the point further. Instead he said slowly, 'You have made a great effort to become one of us, Señorita Lennox. I cannot make up my mind whether this is because you are very generous or very calculating.'

So she was Señorita Lennox again, thought Julia in despair. That was a bad sign. Over the last days he had called her nothing at all except once or twice when, preoccupied and unwontedly friendly, he had used her christian name.

She said lightly, 'By its nature, that's not something I can usefully comment on.'

He raised the dark brows at her.

'Because you wouldn't believe me,' she went on helpfully. 'No matter what I say, or how much I protest that I like the villagers who have been kind to me, you'll discount it all the time if you really think I'm calculating. Won't you?'

Roberto sighed. 'You are too clever. It does not help——'

'Help?'

He shrugged. 'Help me make up my mind about you.'

Julia bit her lip, oddly hurt. 'No, I suppose not,' she said in a subdued voice.

They walked in silence for several minutes. The incline was steep and Julia had to bend her head and breathe carefully in order to avoid her heart racing. Because of the altitude, she told herself, not because of Roberto Madariaga's brooding presence beside her.

He said abruptly, 'For instance, all this looking at watercourses. I do not know what to make of it.'

Julia looked at him, puzzled. Whatever he might think of her motives, she did not think there was much to wonder at about her activities.

She said, 'Do you think I'd poison the water supply or something?' sarcastically.

'No.' His eyes gleamed down at her. She did not think he was laughing at the feeble joke. 'No. But you could be—doing other things as well.'

'Oh yes? Building bonfires to tell passing aircraft where I am? Writing "Help" in letters half a mile across to attract their attention?' Julia spoke nastily because she had a sudden unwelcome realisation that she could very easily break down into tears.

'No, you are not as unrealistic as that. In fact you're a very cool lady,' Roberto said with grudging admiration. 'No tears, no hysterics, right from the first, though you are intelligent enough to know that you could be in real danger. And to seize your chance when I was stupid enough to give it to you,' he added bitterly. 'No, I know you pretty well by now, Julia Lennox. You are cool, clever and very courageous.' He paused and then added with devastating effect, 'That is why I don't trust you.'

She turned her head away from him. His words frightened her, she was not quite sure why. She felt pleased yet hurt at the same time, confused and desperately aware of him. He would only have to reach out his hand six inches or so to take hold of hers and he would know at once how aware of him she was, in every nerve and muscle. She was shaking with the intensity of it. She was terrified that he would reach out across that little space. She moved further away from his side.

'Obviously,' she agreed in a brittle voice.

'For instance,' he went on, ignoring her comment, 'on the one hand, you might be using your undoubted skills to try to help the people here. You are not the first person to observe that there must be a problem of drainage, but you are the first one with the relevant skills to spend time here. On the other hand——'

'Yes?' prompted Julia, not much above a whisper. She had a feeling that she did not want to know what he thought might be her alternative objective.

'Well, you are free and unsupervised on these rambles of yours. You could be making a map of the terrain. Preparing,' he explained with a bleak smile, 'for a more considered escape bid.'

Julia took a deep breath. 'Do you think that's likely?'

Roberto frowned. 'I don't know.' His mouth twisted. 'I know it is not beyond you.' He stopped suddenly and, fearing that he might touch her, she stopped too and turned defensively towards him. His eyes searched her face. 'Which is the truth, Julia?' he asked softly.

She shrugged. 'As I said, only you can decide that.'

He gave an impatient sigh, pushing the hair back off his face with an angry movement.

'I know, I know. And only I can decide what to do about it.'

'Do?' She was startled. Her eyes met his in sudden question.

'Yes, they have to stop, these solitary walks of yours,' he said, in answer to that question. 'There are not enough people in the fields to—watch you.'

Julia digested this in silence. It was a bitter disappointment. 'Does that mean that I have to stop looking at the drainage system?'

'No. But you must always be with someone else.'

She flinched. 'You really mistrust me, don't you?'

His face tensed. 'Not entirely.'

'No? Then why keep me under escort all day?' A thought occurred to her. 'Is that why you're here now? On sentry duty?'

For a moment there was silence while Roberto glared at her. Julia stood before him, tense with defiance, her hair shaken back over her shoulders, her hands clenching in nervous anger.

He said, 'What do you mean?'

'Well, I haven't seen much of you during the day before have I? Not until you came to give me this

instruction that I spend the rest of my time under guard.'
She shook her head in impotent fury. 'Armed guard, no
doubt.'

Roberto's face was masklike. 'Very probably.'

Julia caught her breath in an angry laugh. It was
almost a sob. 'Oh, how I loathe you!'

'I am well aware of that.' A muscle moved in the
otherwise immobile face. She watched fascinated at the
revealing convulsive movement.

She said in swift compunction, 'I'm sorry, I didn't
mean it—I was on edge.' She spread her hands
appealingly. 'But try to see it from my point of view.'

He gave a harsh laugh. 'I have to see it from everyone's
point of view. And what I see, I don't like.'

She looked away, not understanding him but detecting
criticism. 'I have to have something to do,' she said a
little desperately. 'Surely you can understand that? I'll go
mad if I have to sit here and twiddle my thumbs all day!
Especially as I don't know what's going on. I don't even
know where you are,' she ended on a bitter note.

Roberto looked at her narrowly. 'That is important to
you?'

'It does not make me feel any safer,' Julia told him,
after a tiny pause.

'Ah, your safety—of course.' He frowned. 'Well, there
is a remedy. I had thought of it before, but it seemed too
fraught—on a number of counts. Maybe I was wrong.'

Julia stared. 'What are you talking about?'

'My travels which leave you alone all day,' he told her
blandly. 'From now on, I will not neglect you so
shamefully.' And, as apprehension flared in her eyes, he
nodded. 'Yes. You will come with me.'

CHAPTER SIX

HE put his threat—for so she interpreted it—into practice at once. The very next day, in fact, he shook her awake.

'What is it?' murmured Julia sleepily. For a confused moment she thought she was back, geographically and in time, in her student days in Edinburgh. 'Hugh?' she said, puzzled.

'No.' The single word was clipped.

Her eyes flew open. Roberto was standing beside the bed already fully dressed in corded breeches and riding boots, a dark handkerchief knotted round his throat, his brown cotton shirt buttoned up to the neck against the early morning cold.

Still half dazed by sleep, Julia smiled. 'You look like a cowboy,' she told him softly.

For just an instant the hazel eyes blazed. Then the fire was blanked out, he was master of himself again and saying coolly, 'Me? Or this—Hugh?'

He sounded bored and faintly contemptuous. Julia came fully awake, struggling to sit up while still keeping the bedclothes modestly disposed around her. Roberto watched her manoeuvres with distant amusement.

She said, stuttering a little in confusion, 'I'm sorry. You—you startled me. I was still half asleep. What—what do you want?'

'Now there's a question!' The amusement deepened. 'At the moment, for you to get up and get dressed so that we can set off.'

'Oh.' She swallowed nervously. 'Oh yes, of course.' She did not make a move. She could not, while he stood there watching her like that. 'Where—where are we going?'

'If I told you, you wouldn't be any the wiser. And it's probably better if you don't know, anyway. That way you won't have to keep any secrets.'

'You don't trust me,' said Julia, surprised how much the discovery hurt.

'I don't trust anybody,' Roberto said with sudden harshness. 'Least of all women who lie in bed and flutter their eyelashes at me. Are you going to get up, or do I have to dress you personally?'

Julia flushed but said with dignity, 'I'll get up as soon as you leave me to do so in decent privacy.'

His eyebrows flew up. 'How very modest! How very unexpected.' He shrugged. 'But it shall be as you wish. Be outside in ten minutes, though, or I *will* dress you myself.'

As soon as the door shut behind him, Julia flung herself out of the bed, the coverlets trailing on the floor. and began pulling on her borrowed clothes with feverish haste! She had no doubt at all that he would fulfil his threat if she did not comply.

Outside, he was waiting with two horses, sturdy rather than beautiful beasts, standing placidly in the half dark at the end of the street. Julia went up to them noiselessly, shivering a little, in spite of her tightly buttoned shirt and jacket. Roberto looked at her frowning faintly.

'Is that all you're going to wear? We're going up, you know. You'll freeze.'

Julia shook her head. 'I haven't anything else. And all of this belongs to Marta.'

He made a sound of impatience and disappeared briefly back to the hut. When he returned it was with an oddly shaped grey and cream wool garment. At first she thought it was a blanket, but then he spread it out and she could see a vestigial neckline.

'Poncho,' he said succinctly. 'Not as bright as the Mexican ones, but it will keep you warm.' Before she knew what he was about he had thrown it deftly over her head. It fell to her hips, covering her arms entirely, so that she had no freedom of movement at all. It was an odd sensation, but she felt the return of warmth immediately.

'Thank you,' she said with unfeigned gratitude.

For a moment he looked down at her, his hands hard on her wool-covered arms. Then he shrugged, turning to his horse and unlooping the rein.

'I hope you can ride.'

'If not, I'm in for an uncomfortable time,' agreed Julia drily.

He gave a short bark of laughter. 'You're in for an uncomfortable time anyway! These are mountain tracks we are travelling on. It's no riding school trot round a flat field.'

They set off, Julia scrambling on to the back of her mount as best she could, Roberto vaulting easily into the saddle. The horses' hooves made an eerie clipping noise as they rode out of the sleeping village. As much to break the disturbing silence as anything, Julia asked, 'How do you know about riding school trots? Is that how you learned to ride?'

He threw her a wry look. 'I don't remember learning to ride. I had a horse as soon as I could stand, more or less. My father loved horses, and anyway, it was the only method of reaching some of the remoter parts of our estates.'

Julia digested this in silence. The little remark conjured up a picture of a childhood almost unimaginably different from her own.

'Were you close to your father?' she asked, unaware of the wistfulness in her voice, though the man gave her a searching look before he answered.

'We were reasonably good friends. Mine is not a family which encourages closeness.'

Julia gave a little shiver. That, at least, she recognised.

'I went away to school,' he went on, after a pause. 'My mother sent us all away. It was supposed to teach us independence.' His tone was neutral.

'And did it?' she asked.

He shrugged. 'I don't think independence is something that can be taught. Some people just are—the cold ones. Like my mother,' he added meditatively, 'and I think maybe you!'

Julia did not answer. His remark saddened her. Perhaps that was how she appeared to strangers these days, cold and aloof in her independence.

At length she said softly, 'And you?'

'Me?' He seemed startled.

'Did you not achieve this independence your mother wanted?' She paused before adding deliberately, 'And the coldness?'

He gave a low laugh. 'Are you challenging me?'

'What?' She was confused and thoroughly thrown off balance by the swift reply.

'Maybe not deliberately. But I will remind you of that, some time in the future.' He sounded amused, more relaxed. She did not understand him but was relieved that he no longer seemed so harsh. He went on, 'I suppose I rather enjoyed my odd schooling. I have always liked travel, It was different for my brother and sisters, though. For them it was a mistake, as my mother now realises. She is trying to make amends, too, but it is a little late in the day.'

Julia nodded. 'Marta told me.' She remembered that he had agreed to end his love affair with Florita in order to make a home for the rest of his family and watched him speculatively. He did not sound bitter. Perhaps he was a man to whom lovers were only of passing interest anyway. A man like Roberto Madariaga would have more important things to do than commit himself to a woman. The thought hurt, for some reason, and she felt that deep sadness touch at her again.

'Did she?' He was quite indifferent to being gossiped about. Presumably he was used to it. 'Her family have worked for us for many years. Her father was the estate manager and, in the last years, my father's best friend.'

'Is that why she's here up in the mountains with you?' asked Julia, as it suddenly occurred to her that Marta, more serious and less flamboyant than her beautiful sister, might be exactly the sort of wife that Doña Eleanora would think suitable for her son.

Roberto tensed. 'Yes,' he said evenly, 'I bear that responsibility, too, along with all the others.'

Oddly, it hurt to have her suspicion confirmed. Julia looked away towards the east where the first lines of dawn were streaking the sky dramatically.

He said, almost to himself, 'If there is bloodshed, I will bear a very heavy burden.'

She gave him a quick look and would have answered, but at that point the path began to climb steeply as it narrowed and she had to pull her horse in behind his and follow him at a cautious distance to avoid the little pebbles that were dislodged by his horse's hooves. Further conversation was impossible and remained so until they came in sight of a little town, nestling among the peaks in a narrow valley.

Roberto slowed his horse so that she could catch up with him. With some difficulty—since she had ridden only a couple of times in her life and the beast she was riding had a will of its own—Julia did so.

'I do not think anyone will ask you about yourself,' Roberto told her. 'As you are with me, they would think it a discourtesy. If by some chance somebody does, however, say as little as possible. Pretend your Spanish is limited, or something.'

Julia looked at him curiously. 'Would they harm me if they knew who I was and where I came from?'

His face darkened, but at length he said heavily, 'I just do not know. If you had asked me that three years ago— or even three months—I would have laughed at the idea

of any of these people hurting a fly. Now, I'm not sure of
anything any more.'

Julia said very quietly, 'Hadn't you better tell me how
matters stand?' And when he said nothing, she added on
a little spurt of anger, 'For your safety if not for mine.'

He transferred the reins to one hand and palmed his
eyes as if they were hurting him. For the first time Julia
realised how tired he looked, as if he were being stretched
tauter and tauter to the point where there would be no
bearing it. He seemed as if he was holding on to his calm
by a thread now, while they were alone, but she was
certain that when they rode into that little town and were
surrounded by people for whom he felt responsible, he
would be his public self again, assured, confident of
success. Yet he must be holding down this tension, this
anxiety, all the time. Her respect for him grew in that
moment.

She said more gently, 'It sometimes helps to share
things, you know.'

Roberto gave a laugh which was more than half a
groan. 'I have been trying very hard not to share, don't
you realise that? It can only put you in greater danger
than you are now.'

'That's just your opinion. You can't be sure of it.
Anyway, I'll risk it.'

'You don't know what you're saying. you don't know
the risks . . .'

'No,' said Julia, 'I don't. And that's what scares me.'

He brought the horses to a halt and swung round to
look deep into her eyes. Then he gave a long sigh, as if a
burden had slid off his shoulders.

'Very well. You have the right to choose, I suppose.'

'Thank you,' she said with irony, but gently.

He shrugged. 'Well, you might not have wanted that
right. My mother, who is very insistent on getting her
own way, is equally insistent on not being told anything
uncomfortable. And this,' he added grimly, 'is a damned

sight more than that. It is downright dangerous.'

'So is ignorance,' said Julia. 'And I wish you would stop judging me by your mother, whom I've never met.'

Roberto smiled faintly. 'You will,' he said, to her surprise and consternation. 'But maybe you're right.'

'I am,' she said sturdily. 'So tell me, who is fighting whom? And whose side are we on?'

He looked slightly startled. 'You're not on anybody's side. You're here by accident.'

She looked down at her hands, discomfited. 'Oh. Yes, of course.'

'That's important,' he said urgently. 'You're nothing to do with me except the spoils of war. You must remember that.'

It hurt—it hurt horribly. But she managed to nod her head in an intelligent manner and maintain a calm look of interest.

He went on wearily, 'The country has been sewn up by the military for years. The present General—your President Valetta to whom you were going to sell your company's services—is just the last in a long line of generals. And the greediest.'

'I believe that,' said Julia, remembering.

'It came to my attention last year that he was—how shall I put it—building up a surprisingly large bank account in Switzerland. He has bought a house there too. I came home and made some discreet enquiries—and found that almost the entire country was united in opposition to him.'

'So why don't you simply kick him out?' asked Julia, the democrat.

Roberto smiled wryly. 'I should have said the entire country apart from the Air Force. He may not be popular, but he is very well armed, which is not a bad substitute.'

'But if he's building up a Swiss bank account, he must be expecting to be kicked out of the country at some point,' observed Julia.

Roberto's eyes narrowed. 'You're very shrewd. He is, of course, but by another military rival. My object—and my friends' object—is to make sure that he goes, and when he goes that there are proper elections.'

'And will he go?'

'I think so. I think he has seen the end of the road for some time, as you so acutely deduced. That is not really the problem.'

'Then what is?' asked Julia as he seemed to withdraw inside himself, the tense, brooding look that tore at her heart beginning to shadow his face.

Roberto shook himself, coming out of his brown study. 'My allies, rather than my enemy, I'm afraid. There are just too many of them and they all want to rule their little bit of the country. That is the ones that don't want to rule all of it. Some of them are violent, some of them are crooks, some of them are starry-eyed young political thugs. Most of them have been involved in a struggle against the government for years, whereas I am not only one of the suspect landed classes but I've only been back from abroad for a few months.' He sighed. 'Oh, I understand their reasoning, even sympathise with some of them. It doesn't make any difference to the fact that the most important job is to unite them and that nobody but me seems inclined to try.'

'I see.' Julia shivered, though the sun was now high.

He looked at her sharply. 'Do you? Do you really? Do you understand how precarious my position is?' He leaned forward suddenly, taking her chin between ungentle fingers and turning her to face him. 'Do you understand that I *cannot* guarantee your safety?' He sounded furious.

She met his eyes squarely, a faint smile in her own, 'You've made it very clear. I'll be careful, I promise.' She put up her hand and gently detached his fingers. 'What are we doing here? Chatting up another of your slippery allies?'

'That's it.' He took up the reins again and gave them a little shake. At the sign both horses began to move forward, surprising Julia so that she had to make a grab at the mane of her own horse before she regained her balance. Roberto was staring straight ahead between his horse's ears and did not notice. 'We have not got long now,' he said almost to himself. 'The President is ready to talk. And if we do not speak with one voice, then there will be another military coup, another general, another cycle of greed and repression.'

'And you think you can stop it?' asked Julia, watching the firm profile.

He closed his eyes briefly, as if against a light which hurt them. 'I don't know. I know I have to try.'

She would have liked to say something supportive, to touch him, but she did not dare.

She did say, quietly, 'You're very brave.'

He gave a harsh laugh. 'I'm very reckless. That's what my mother says, and she's not wrong. Only it has to be done. But sometimes—when it's other people's lives I'm gambling with—I wonder whether it's worth it, whether I've made the right choice.'

Julia said, 'And I haven't helped.'

'Dear God, no!' he said with unmistakable feeling. 'It has been a thousandfold worse since——'

She flinched, though he broke off what he was going to say before he could be insulting.

She said stiffly, 'I will keep out of the way, I promise.'

She was as good as her word. She trailed silently behind him throughout the visit, responding to courtesies and queries alike with a smile and a few laboured words of Spanish which made it clearer than any explanations that she did not speak their language. And Roberto made it clear, without any words at all, that she was his lady and was there for his loving. It made Julia feel oddly cherished, although it was all pretence.

When they rode back, Roberto barely spoke to her, though he congratulated her quietly on her discretion. She thanked him curtly. She was very tired after the unaccustomed exercise and she had an odd, unreasonable black mood on her that made her want to creep away from him and cry.

By the time they reached the village, she was so beaten by exhaustion, she preceded him into the little house without a shred of embarrassment. She was swaying where she stood. Silently he made her sit down and drew off her boots.

'You're asleep on your feet,' he said abruptly. 'I've done that to you, as well, haven't I?'

Julia shook her head wearily, not understanding.

'Stand up.'

She did so, her eyelids falling helplessly, though she tried to keep them open. Calmly, impersonally, he took off her clothes, supporting her with one arm as he did so. She swung in his indifferent embrace like a limp marionette. He pulled one of his shirts over her head. It smelled deliciously of herbs and the sun in which it had dried. Drowsily she turned her head into her shoulder, inhaling.

'Nice,' she murmured.

'You're—dangerous,' he said in a strained voice she barely recognised.

He swung her off her feet, easily, and deposited her in the bed which someone, probably Angelina, had made in their absence. He pulled the bedclothes up to her chin and held them there, none too gently. She murmured a protest, turning towards him in her half-sleep.

'Oh no.' He was grim. 'I have work to do and,' his voice sank to a sharp whisper, 'anyway, I'm not Hugh, whoever he may be. When I take you to bed, it won't be because you're lonely for another man!'

The door slammed behind him.

The days that followed were all on the same pattern. They would ride out together before it was light, sometimes riding five or six hours before they reached their destination. There Julia could watch and see for herself the truth of what Roberto had told her about the uneasy alliance of which he was part. Though on the whole the men he spoke to seemed to trust him, they had harsh words for the others of their number. In particular there was a bandit in the hills whom they all seemed to fear.

She asked about him one day, and Roberto was thoughtful.

'Why do you bring up his name?'

'Because everyone else does,' Julia said with pardonable exasperation. 'As if he were Captain Bligh, or something.'

'He's a villain,' Roberto said calmly. 'Given my choice I'd have nothing to do with him. But the headmen in the villages to the north are terrified of him and won't support us unless I can at least guarantee that Augusto will not take it in bad part.'

'Will you have to see him?' she asked, her heart sinking.

'I shall try, in any event.' He smiled. 'I have been into his territory several times, but he always has just left. I've never known Augusto be so elusive before. Normally he just shoots it out.'

'Don't make jokes about it!' Julia cried sharply.

Roberto looked surprised. 'Very well, since it alarms you. But you must see that it has its funny side.'

'No.' She sat straight-backed on her mare. 'No, I don't see that at all.'

She saw it even less as they rode into the village. An ugly piebald horse with a mean eye was tethered to the veranda of Angelina's house.

'Well, well!' Roberto gave a soft whistle. 'Mahomet has come to the mountain, it seems.'

'What do you mean?' demanded Julia, full of apprehension.

He swung off his horse, shaking the dark hair out of his eyes and giving her one of his rare, dazzling smiles.

'I mean, my dear Julia, that you are about to meet your first double-dyed bandit.'

He strolled into the house, reaching out an imperative hand behind him for her to follow. Obediently, she slid her hand into his, noting how cold her skin felt against the warm muscle and bone of his own.

As they walked in, three men who were sitting round Angelina's table looked up. Roberto stopped, though he did not stop smiling.

'Gentlemen,' he acknowledged them. His eyes went round the table. 'Good evening Miguel. I did not expect to see you away from your patients this evening. Señor Borsa, how pleasant to meet you again after—what is it?—only two days? And,' his voice lowered blandly, 'my old friend Augusto. Were you waiting for me?'

The one called Augusto was swarthy and, in Julia's opinion, rather dirty. He was of an unimpressive height and girth beside Roberto and Miguel Olivados, whom she had met. Even the elephantine Borsa was more imposing. But the bandit had a wolfish quality that frightened her. In Roberto's her fingers twitched. Unseen, he clasped them tightly for a moment in a reassuring squeeze.

'I was,' the bandit snarled. 'I've wanted to see you for days while you've been taking your foreign bit of skirt sightseeing over my country!'

Julia knew, she did not know how, that Roberto was angry. But he said evenly, 'And I have wanted to see you, my dear Augusto.'

'Yes?' The bandit sounded sceptical.

'Naturally. As I understand we are on the same side.'

'I'm on my own side,' said Augusto with a coarse laugh. 'I don't need you, Madariaga.'

'Then why are you here?' asked Roberto in an idle tone.

He took Julia's hand and carried it to his mouth, as if it was something that he did frequently, absentmindedly. As he feathered kisses across the knuckles he watched the bandit unwaveringly. Julia trembled but stood quiet.

'I hear from Alto Rio that Valetta has agreed to talk,' Augusto said abruptly. 'Is it true?'

Roberto was calm. 'Yes.'

'The Air Force agree?'

'I doubt whether they know,' Roberto said tranquilly.

The bandit gave a burst of loud laughter. 'If they find out they'll blast you out of the mountains!'

'They are not going to find out. And I doubt if they could find us.'

Augusto's little eyes shifted restlessly about the room. 'Who is she?' he demanded, indicating Julia with a jerk of the head.

Roberto smiled, drawing her forward, and running a possessive hand over her hip.

'You've never lacked for that,' agreed Augusto, unimpressed. 'But why a foreigner? Why *now*? Who is she?'

Miguel Olivados, a thin-faced, earnest man, younger than the bandit, possibly even younger than Roberto, protested, 'Do we ask you about your women, my friend?'

Augusto shrugged. The air was full of menace. 'I think you are trying to double cross me, *Don* Roberto,' he sneered.

'I don't play such games with experts,' Roberto answered, and Julia watched the man's face darken as he understood the insult. He went on, 'What do you want, Augusto? Presumably not to waste my time speculating about my private life.'

'If you're meeting Valetta, I've got a right to be there.'
'Possibly.'

Julia stared at him. He sounded unconvinced, yet he
had told her more or less that Augusto's participation
was vital. Then she understood what he was doing. If he
seemed too eager, the bandit would lose interest or
become suspicious. If he seemed unconvinced the bandit
would be determined to make his point.

'I'll be there, Madariaga,' Augusto told him veno-
mously, 'or there'll be no meeting.'

'We'll think about it.' Roberto nodded to Miguel.
'There are more to be consulted than just myself, you
understand.'

The bandit looked contemptuous. 'Oh, of course—
Roberto Madariaga, the divine democrat. Did you have
a referendum before you took *her* into your bed?' he
sneered. 'Well, take your votes, if you want, but I warn
you I'll be there.'

'I'm sure you will.' Roberto was placatory. 'And very
welcome.'

Augusto sat down suddenly on a wooden bench.
'You're a weak man, Madariaga. you think you're so
brave with your French degrees and your American
friends, but out here you're nothing. Pouf!' And he
snapped his fingers.

'Where men are men,' murmured Roberto in amusement, but Augusto, calling rudely for rum, did not hear
him. Olivados did, though, and sent him a look of
anguished warning. 'You may be right, Augusto, I'm
certainly not used to riding sixty kilometres a day.'

'Have I kept you too long out of your bed, Madariaga?'
sneered Augusto, with a look at Julia which turned her
blood to ice.

Roberto, however, was unmoved. 'Much too long,' he
said coolly. He turned away, saying over his shoulder,
'When I have talked to the others Borsa can bring you
their answer. In the meantime, I shall continue to

negotiate with Valetta. And I shall know if you try to betray us, Augusto. And so will the others!' he ended, with unmistakable threat.

He marched Julia out of the house without bothering to say goodnight. It was cold outside. Julia felt it strike against her skin, as she put up a hand to her hot cheek.

Roberto said remotely, 'I'm sorry about that. I warned you what might happen one day. Augusto was coming round to demanding to take you into the hills with him as a hostage. Borsa would have supported him, and I could not risk that. I had to tell him you were my woman.'

Julia said, 'So I inferred. I'm almost becoming used to it.'

She moved a little away from him. She had known there was something behind his sudden display of affection. Why did it hurt to know what it was?

'You are a remarkable woman,' Roberto told her after a pause. He made no move to touch her. 'I imagine I do not need to tell you to be careful to maintain this—fiction—of mine?'

'I can see that it provides my best chance of safety,' she agreed with assumed serenity. 'Rely on me. If asked, I shall say I'm desperately in love.'

Roberto gave a crack of laughter. 'I'm sorry to disillusion you, but I doubt whether they give a damn about what you may or may not feel. You'll do much better to assure them that *I* am desperately in love.'

They had reached the house. He pushed the door open for her, and followed her in, closing it behind him. He went down on his haunches, apparently feeling for a bolt, and she heard him swear softly.

'What is it?' she asked.

'The bolt has rusted,' he said in disgust. 'One good push and it will come away—look.'

She did so. The catch was flaking with rust and attached to the door frame by only one insecure-looking nail.

'I see what you mean.' She looked down at his head, disturbed. 'But does it matter? I mean, nobody steals things here . . .'

He gave an impatient sigh. 'It matters if we are to protect our privacy. And protecting our privacy, may I remind you, means protecting *you.*'

Julia swallowed, suddenly cold again. 'You think someone will come in?'

'I think it may occur to Augusto to do a little checking up,' Roberto said grimly. 'He is not sure about me and he sure as hell does not trust a foreign woman with international money behind her. Oh,' in a sudden rush of exasperation, 'go to bed! Whatever he has in mind, he can hardly do anything tonight.'

'No,' Julia agreed doubtfully. 'I—I mean, will you— that is, do you intend to stay here?'

Roberto stood up and gave her an incredulous look. 'Tonight? Of course.'

'I see.' She looked away, horribly aware of constricting shyness and furious with herself. 'Then I'll go to bed,' she said, trying for nonchalance.

'Do that.' He sounded weary. 'I must do some work, but I will try not to disturb you.' He turned away, nodding to her almost absently. His mind, she thought, was already on his work. 'Goodnight.'

She undressed swiftly and as modestly as possible, standing in the lee of the chest of drawers. Her precautions were unnecessary; Roberto was hunched over the desk, concentrating on the papers before him and he never once looked round. She shrugged herself into the shirt of his that she had borrowed to sleep in and slid under the covers. He did not notice.

For a long time, it seemed, Julia lay on her side, her head slightly tipped back on the pillow, watching him. He was oblivious. It gave her full opportunity to study the beautiful, uncompromising profile, the way the dark hair curled forward on to his neck, the long-fingered elegance of his hands.

Her stomach clenched and she gave a little shiver. She could fall in love with those hands. If she was not so wise, so cautious, and if she did not have the experience to teach her that love was a fool's game, she just possibly might—for a little while—find peace and pleasure and comfort with this man.

In spite of herself, her eyes kept closing. Several images of him danced in her brain, images of him as she had never seen him: kind and loving and drowning in passion. She began to drift into a dream. Her hand slipped under her cheek and she turned her head into the pillow with a soft sigh which did at last, though she did not know it, bring Roberto's eyes round to her sleeping form.

He watched her without expression from his vantage point by the desk. Once she stirred and murmured in her sleep and at once he tensed. But she fell quiet again. He stood up and went to look down at her. She had pushed the covers away from one shoulder. Very gently he drew them back over her body, holding them in place for an instant before turning sharply, almost flinging himself away, back to his seat at the desk and the study of his maps.

Julia slept lightly, troubled by dreams. Something was missing, she had lost it, it was her fault and her life would finish if she could not find it. There was darkness all round her, full of hidden obstacles, and she was being chased. She was afraid; she wanted to cry out. But she could not cry out, Roberto had told her not to. It would put him in terrible danger if she cried out.

She threshed her way out of the dream, panting, to hear Roberto's voice saying with a hushed urgency that was the reverse of soothing, 'Hush! For God's sake, hush, my darling.'

Julia froze. It was absolutely dark in the little house.

The reading lamp by the light of which he had been working had been doused. He appeared to be lying beside her, one arm across her body pinning her to the bed. He was not looking at her, though. His head was turned in straining attitude towards the window and he appeared to be listening.

Julia moistened her dry lips. 'What is it?' she whispered in his ear.

'I'm not sure.' He was as quiet as she. 'I thought I heard something. Maybe we're being watched—in which case. I've been a fool.'

'A fool?'

Roberto turned his head and looked down at her. She could make out the glitter of his eyes in the darkness.

'I told them I couldn't wait to get you into bed,' he said deliberately. 'I shouldn't have sat up reading if I wanted them to believe me.'

'Oh!' Julia felt fear touch her but, oddly, it was not as acute as it had been earlier. Lying close to Roberto like this, breathing her words into his ear was comforting, she found; even pleasurable. 'Then why did you?'

'It never occurred to me that Augusto might spy on us tonight. I thought he would ride straight back to his camp. I,' said Roberto bitterly, 'am a fool.'

She freed a hand and ran it over his dark hair.

'You can't think of everything. Don't blame yourself.'

'And that bloody door is not secure either,' he said, ignoring her words and her gesture.

Julia made a decision.

'Where is he?' she asked.

'Augusto? Outside under the window.' Roberto looked back towards the shutters. 'He won't be able to see anything; he has no light. But he's there listening and he has hearing like a cat.' He sounded despairing.

Julia was quite calm. 'Then we'd better give him something to listen to,' she said, her lips moving against his ear 'You've finished your work, you've come to bed and now you're going to make love to me. All perfectly plausible.' She moved. freeing her arm from the covers and embracing him. 'Darling,' she said louder, in a breathless tone of absolute longing, 'oh, darling . . .'

For a moment, to her consternation, she thought Roberto was going to push her away. He drew a sharp breath and seemed as if he was going to protest. But then he relaxed, giving a soft laugh, and his hand began to move in her hair.

He made love to her in Spanish, presumably for the benefit of their unseen auditor. That chilled her, even as she moved in his arms, inviting his kisses and the soft murmured words of love.

'*Adorada—mi amor.*' There was a faint undertone of laughter in his voice which Julia hoped desperately did not reach the listening bandit. She could hear nothing from the window, though she strained her ears.

Roberto was pushing the covers away from her. She stiffened but, realising that it was for the benefit of their audience, relaxed and even aided him. He laughed softly and brushed a kiss across her lips.

When the covers had gone, sliding eventually on to the floor, Roberto paused. Propping himself on one elbow, he seemed to be looking down at her, though in the darkness she could not be quite sure. He could have been looking inward, debating with himself. Again she felt that little shiver of alienation. It was wrong, Julia thought suddenly, wrong to be in bed with this man without love or the mutual freedoms of lovers.

She said hesitantly, 'Roberto . . .'

His only answer was to brush the hair gently off her face. For some moments he did not speak, simply resting beside her, stroking her hair, running a gentle forefinger over her brow and nose and mouth. It made her feel like a petted cat and was inexplicably moving.

Then he said, almost absently, '*Sí?*'

Julia gave a breathless laugh. 'If you keep doing that I

shall start to purr!'

His eyes gleamed down at her. 'Will you?' His thumb
caressed her bottom lip, stayed there. 'I think I might like
that.'

Julia went very still under his hand. It seemed to her
that he was waiting for something, she was not sure what.
Some noise from outside the window, maybe, or perhaps
even an intrusion into their privacy. It was frustrating
not to be able to ask.

Then he gave a long sigh, shifted his body to a more
comfortable position, trapped her shoulders with one
long arm and bent his head.

As a kiss to deceive a third party it was, Julia thought
in bewilderment, rather excessive. It was also a
revelation.

He was not hurtful but he was very firm. There was no
way she could escape that purposeful mouth, even had
she wanted to. Of course, she did not want to, because
there was the watcher to be considered, she told herself as
her senses swam dizzily and she clung on to him in pure
reflex against the reeling world. The night air was
blisteringly cold, but Julia did not feel it, sheltered and
warmed by the length of a strong body. She began to
tremble, though.

Roberto lifted his head. 'Purring?' he murmured, still
laughing.

Julia's throat was dry with unfamiliar sensations, but
she managed to whisper, 'If you like.'

'Oh, I do.' He dipped his head and ran his tongue
briefly between her lips, giving a soft chuckle when she
shuddered in uncontrollable response. 'I like it very
much; can't you tell?'

She said demurely, 'I don't know you well enough to
draw conclusions about what you like and what you don't
like.'

He said caressingly against her skin, 'You're a liar. Of
course you know. All women know.'

'Do they?' Julia said sadly, thinking of Florita who was so beautiful and glamorous and of all the other women in his life. There must have been so many of them.

'Of course,' Roberto murmured, his mouth moving along the line of her shoulder, pushing away his shirt from the satin-smooth skin.

She touched his crisp hair fleetingly, tentatively, alarmed almost at her own daring.

'Roberto—I——' She broke off with a gasp as his teeth nipped sensuously at the skin he had exposed.

'Hmm?' It was the softest of sounds, a bare acknowledgement that she had spoken. He was concentrating all his attention on the revealing reflexes of her body. Their responsiveness appeared to please him. He dusted kisses along her collarbone, saying absently, 'Yes?'

Julia realised, blindingly, that she had never felt like this before. Even Hugh, whom she had thought she had loved, had never inspired her with this trembling, this exquisite anticipation, this sense of impending abandonment. She forgot the watcher at the window.

She said gravely, not as a warning but somehow because it was important that he should know the truth, 'Roberto, I don't go in for one-night stands.'

He gave a soft laugh, not raising his head. 'Not a pretty phrase that! And I never said you did.'

His lips reached the inside of her elbow, infinitely warm and gentle, and Julia shook convulsively at the touch.

'I mean it,' she insisted in a breathless voice.

'I believe you.' He was quite indifferent it seemed. He began to outline the curve of her breast thoughtfully with the back of his hand. 'Are you telling me you're a virgin?'

'I——' Julia bit her lip. 'No,' she said at last in a small voice.

Roberto laughed again. 'An honest woman; her price is above rubies,' he said cynically.

Julia flinched. That sardonic note hurt, as so many of the things he said to her hurt. She wondered whether all men of his age and experience shared this disillusion or whether he had been embittered by one particular incident.

She said on a little rush of indignation, 'Does it make that much difference? That I'm not a virgin, I mean.'

'Of course it does,' said Roberto impatiently and added, as she stiffened, 'to both of us.'

And then his hands began to move strongly, moulding her body against his with a negligent power that half dismayed, half enthralled her. He unbuttoned the shirt without once lifting his lips from her skin and eased it away from her.

She said blankly, 'I'll be cold.'

Roberto gave a soft laugh. 'No, you won't—I will see to it. That's a promise.'

He wooed her as if he was engaged in a work of art, taking her from movement to movement with care and exquisite timing. Julia was helpless to do anything but respond as he wanted, as he intended. Where he touched, her skin felt as if it had been turned to silk. When he moved she followed him, echoed him. There was something almost ceremonious about the way he touched her, everywhere, as if he was systematically laying claim to her. The slow spiralling of desire deep within her had her shaking, but Roberto was still, carefully, exploring every part of her.

Julia gasped, her fingers clutching convulsively at his shoulders. He was still fully dressed. Feverishly she began to tug at the buttons of his shirt, and Roberto went still.

Then, slowly, almost menacingly, he covered her hands with his own and trapped them against the hard wall of his chest. His heart was beating deeply, steadily. In contrast to her own, his breathing was not even ruffled.

He said in a neutral voice, as if he was asking her to make a choice between two routes on a map, 'Do you want me?'

Her hands twisted under his but could not get free from that iron hold.

'Yes,' she said harshly, not recognising herself in the naked need she heard in that one word.

'Muy bien.' It was still unemotional, as if he too had made a choice which might easily have been the opposite.

He stood up swiftly and stripped. Julia watched his outline in the darkness. He was fast and efficient but not careless, laying the discarded garments carefully across the back of the chair. The cold night air struck her and she shivered.

When he returned to her, she was already reaching for him, arching her body to his in undisguisable passion. She ran her hands down the long fluid line of his spine and for the first time felt him shudder in his turn. He parted her thighs unhurriedly, and she heard herself moan, not realising she had spoken. Roberto said something, she was not sure what, perhaps it was her name.

Suddenly she realised that the long, languorous wooing of her body was over, that now he was as urgent as she. When his body finally moved into her own she gasped, a little frightened at the intensity of her feelings, the sheer magnitude of what she was doing. And then she forgot everything but Roberto, the sweetness of his strength inside her and the infinite ability that he had to fill her, mind and heart and body, with passion. Tears stung her eyes as she gathered him against her fiercely, aware of the blood thundering in her veins as, inexorably, he impelled her higher and higher up that dark path. She cried out, confused and fearful, but she was in his power and he would not let her falter. Then at last, on a wild surge, she was there, free, soaring with him into darkness and exquisite peace.

Afterwards she lay very still, listening. The air seemed to hum with life, as if music had just died and the soundless vibrations were still around them. She felt calm and yet tingling with life. She sighed softly. It was no more than a breath, but Roberto, now utterly attuned to her, heard it. Or perhaps he felt it. He was lying on his back; he had not spoken. Now he reached out an arm and put it round her, drawing her against his shoulder.

With another sigh of pure satisfaction, Julia dropped her head on to his chest, curled against him, and fell into the deepest, sweetest sleep of her life.

CHAPTER SEVEN

IN the morning he was gone. There was no note, nothing, to say where or why or when he would return. Just the absence of his clothes, his binoculars and a map.

Julia did not quite believe it. She wandered blankly round the little house looking for some sort of sign that last night they had been lovers, that he cared. And found nothing.

At last she gave up. She tidied the house, though in his brief visit Roberto had displaced nothing. Except my whole life, thought Julia, with painful irony. There was a little ache in her body this morning which she could not ignore. When she looked in the spotted mirror, though, she seemed the same. There was no outward sign that last night Roberto Madariaga had made her his for all time.

She gave a little superstitious shudder at the thought. It was nonsense, she told herself with resolution. One night's pleasure did not deliver you body and soul into the domination of another human being. Certainly Roberto did not feel that he had surrendered his happiness to her because of last night; the empty house was sufficient evidence of that.

Julia shrugged. She would not think about it. She had had plenty of practice in controlling her emotions which she could call on. She had learned to forgive her aunt and uncle for their cold unkindness. She had, eventually, forgotten Hugh's crueller friendly indifference. She realised, with a slight shock, that she could barely remember his face today. So she had not only got over that blow, she must have forgiven Hugh too.

She would use the same disciplines now. She would ignore Roberto, put the thought of him out of her mind.

She would work until she was so tired she fell asleep where she stood. There would be no leaving herself time to daydream about him. That, she knew from experience, would be fatal. And she was not dissolving into tears over Roberto Madariaga until she was out of his country and safe in her own home again.

Julia straightened her shoulders and went out into the glare of the morning sun, looking for work.

It was easy enough to think what to do. She had not yet been to the fields a little upstream to the north which were shadowed steeply by the peaks above them. She took the little scribbler pad she had started to carry with her from the pocket of her jeans and made a note of the date, approximate time and start of her investigative expedition. Then she set off.

It took her an hour and a half to walk. She guessed that it would take a villager, used to the height and the uneven terrain, perhaps two-thirds of that. She saw several people she knew who waved to her, but nobody was working in the high fields. She walked round them, measuring them by pacing, drawing out a rough sketch map of the area, its incline and the apparently more fertile patches.

She was absorbed in her task when she heard herself hailed by a masculine voice. For a moment she stiffened, then, realising it was not Roberto, she turned slowly.

Miguel Olivados was coming towards her across the stubble. He moved unhurriedly and seemed friendly enough. Some of her initial wariness was dispelled and she stood up to greet him.

'Angelina told me you were here,' Olivados said, smiling at her. 'What are you doing? Angelina said you were going to make the crops grow. Are you a witch?'

Surprised into amusement, Julia laughed. 'I wish I were! Observations take a lot longer than spells.'

'Ah, I see—you're a professional.' He gave her a measuring look. 'Have you been doing it long?'

Normally, Julia found, new acquaintances expressed disbelief that she could have anything to do with farming. Then they marvelled that any woman could have anything to do with it. This easy acceptance of her professional skills made her warm to him.

'Ever since I left university,' she said, sitting down again on a convenient flat stone. 'Even before, if you count my research.'

'So long?' He was thoughtful, dropping down beside her companionably. 'What do you think of the land here?'

Julia shook her head. 'It's all very impressionistic. I haven't my kit, so I can't tell about acidity. But just on the basis of the geography, I'd say that the drainage was all right until somebody built the dam and canal system I can see to the east.'

Olivados looked interested. 'Do you think so? It was considered a great improvement at the time.'

She shook her head. 'I told you, I can't be sure. I need more time, more tools. And,' she added grimly, 'more freedom.'

She had half expected him to look ashamed, but instead he seemed faintly amused. 'Yes, I'd heard Roberto doesn't like you out of his sight.'

She sniffed, thinking that Roberto had hardly been passionate for her company this morning. But, mindful of his frequent instructions, she said nothing more. Olivados seemed friendly enough, but she was a stranger here and Roberto had convinced her that her safety lay in the populace believing her to be Roberto's lover. So she allowed him to lead the conversation on to other topics, and eventually, to accompany her back to the village.

There she saw Roberto in the distance, always surrounded by people she did not recognise, listening attentively or, every so often, issuing one of those authoritative commands which were instantly obeyed. Conscious of being an intruder and an additional, unwelcome, responsibility, Julia avoided him. Last night had shaken her. She still felt slightly light-headed and unlike herself. She found she did not want to face him.

Eventually, of course, she had to. In the little house, after the communal supper prepared by Angelina, Roberto returned after she had climbed into bed and pulled the covers defensively round herself. From the doorway he regarded her almost wearily.

'So you haven't managed to fall asleep before I got home,' he said sardonically.

Julia raised her head from the pillow indignantly. 'I only left Angelina's five minutes ago. I can't go to sleep the moment my head touches the pillow!'

'Though I'm sure you tried,' Roberto drawled.

'What do you mean?'

He shrugged. 'You've been jumping away from me all evening as if I have bubonic plague. And you gave me a wide berth today, didn't you? Kept out of my way very efficiently.' He strolled forward, slamming the door behind him. 'I get the impression you've had a lot of practice.'

Julia met his eyes. 'Practice at what?'

'Keeping the unwanted lover at arm's length.'

She could not sustain the intensity of those dark eyes. He was obviously furious, though she could not yet guess what had roused his anger. Her eyes fell away.

'I don't know what you mean.'

'Don't you?' Roberto gave an angry laugh, dropping on to the side of the bed and taking her chin between thumb and forefinger, forcing her to look at him. 'Don't you? Well, let me explain. I think you're a cool lady with a delicious body and all the natural urges. But you also have a successful and enjoyable life jetting round the world and a lover would get in the way. So, while you're perfectly prepared to go to bed with a man who attracts you—occasionally—he is not allowed any rights at any other time. Not so much,' he ended savagely, 'as a friendly greeting in the street.'

Julia's face was utterly white. So now she knew what had infuriated him. Having set his brand on her, he resented the fact that she had failed to display his ownership publicly today. A small, tight knot of pain seemed to have gathered in her chest.

Terrified that he would see the pain and interpret it correctly, she lashed out at him, 'You have *no* rights where I'm concerned!'

His mouth was a thin line. 'So you have made very plain.'

'You have not treated me as a friend. How dare you expect,' she mimicked him furiously, '*a friendly greeting*!'

Roberto shook her. 'Last night I was your lover,' he said between his teeth.

She tossed her hair back, hating him. 'No, you weren't. You don't know the meaning of the word. It takes more than one night to make people lovers.'

Too late she realised the trap that she had set for herself. The thin mouth smiled, though the eyes stayed coldly angry. Julia gasped and recoiled as if she had walked into a brick wall.

'It does indeed,' he said silkily.

She said, on an appalled breath, 'Oh God, no!' but he took no notice.

He did not try to bar the door tonight. Nor did he douse the small lamp still burning on his desk where Julia had lit it. He did not seem aware of either of them, looking down at her as if he hated her.

Julia edged away, but the bed was set in a corner and further boxed in by the chest of drawers. There was no escape except past him, and she did not dare to attempt it. She put up futile hands to stop him; she might just as well have tried to stop a tropical storm. He swept her protests aside, seizing both her hands in one powerful one and dragging her across the bed towards him. With his other hand he wrenched at the shirt until its seams tore and its buttons flew off. The material cut painfully into Julia's flesh and she must have made some small sound because he paused.

'Take it off, then,' he said coldly.

She stared at him, mute.

He shrugged. 'Very well.'

Quite deliberately, he set both hands at the gaping neck and wrenched the garment open. Then he pushed it back over her shoulders so that the shirt hung from her elbows. He looked at her without expression, and Julia turned her head away, tasting shame in all its bitterness. How he must despise her to do this to her!

Her throat moved. The laughter, even the near affection, of last night had all gone. Now he was just angry, angry because she had not acknowledged publicly her absolute physical submission to him. Julia was full of grief, but she was also angry in her turn. Whatever her omissions in his eyes, she had done nothing to deserve this icy contempt.

She said bitterly, 'I suppose I needn't ask what you're intending to do?'

Roberto gave a brief unamused laugh. 'To remind you I am your lover, my dear. What else?'

She did look at him then. 'You sicken me,' she said in level tones.

His smile was crooked. 'Hard words, my love. But your body tells a different story.' His eyes swept over her comprehensively and, though she disdained to look down at herself, she knew what he was seeing. 'Doesn't it?'

'You may flatter yourself that that's the case if you choose,' she said with a shrug. 'It makes no difference to the fact that I don't want this. If I have a choice, my choice is no.'

The chilling smile widened. 'Then I shall have to change your mind,' he said, and tipped her back so suddenly on to the bed that she cried out in alarm.

He took no notice, of course; she would hardly have

expected him to. He took no notice of any of her protests, verbal or physical. In the end, to her shame and despair, she was not even protesting any longer. The slow brilliant seduction had done its work too well and she was clinging to him, begging wordlessly to be taken further, higher. Roberto paused, looking down at her, her face trapped between his hands.

His voice was low, intense. It seemed to Julia that he was taunting her.

'Is your choice no? *Is* it?'

She closed her eyes in an agony of need and shame. Roberto's hands clenched in her hair.

'No, look at me,' he insisted and, as she reluctantly complied, he moved inside her so that she shuddered convulsively. 'Tell me *now* what you want.'

If it was mockery it was the cruellest sort. Julia's face lost all colour. But she could not control the headlong rush of her blood to that burning summit and he knew it. She moistened her lips.

'Please,' she said in a dry whisper.

They came, both of them, in a clamour of senses that blinded and deafened her. It was only when he finally rolled away from her that she realised she was breathing in harsh, racking gasps like sobs. Every bone and muscle ached; her lungs hurt; and her throat burned with the effort of suppressing the tears that threatened. She knew by the rhythm of Roberto's breathing that he had fallen asleep, but she lay beside him, wakeful and humiliated.

At last he stirred, turned his head, moved up on to his elbow. Julia knew he was looking at her, but she did not respond, staring up at the reed roof as if she was memorising its pattern. He gave a harsh sigh. Then he swung out of bed and padded across to the light, doused it, picked up his own clothes where he had thrown them and came back to lie down beside her.

In the darkness he put out a hand, almost tentatively, and laid it on her stomach.

'Well?' he said quietly.

Julia did not move. 'I think I hate you,' she said very tiredly, hardly moving her lips.

'I have no doubt of it, my dear,' Roberto said ironically. 'But hate isn't all of it, as you very well know.'

Julia could not deny it, much as she wanted to; especially not after he had made love to her again, making her respond to him until she cried out in wonder. Then, satisfied, he put her away from him and slept dreamlessly till morning.

That, she found, became the pattern of her life for the next few days. By day she toured the fields, looking at crops and hearing about previous harvests, sometimes with Miguel Olivados, sometimes with one of the others when Olivados was inexplicably absent. Roberto she never saw. She assumed that he continued to travel to the outlying town and villages during the day, and could no longer bear to have her with him. During the day.

By night, though, she made love with him in a terrible silent passion without kindness. They were, she sometimes thought in despair, like two wild animals, clawing at each other in a rage to draw blood. The only thing which prevented her total humiliation was the inescapable fact that Roberto was as consumed by it as she was. Though he was cooler to begin with, he always ended in the same frenzy as herself. She thought he hated that loss of control even more than he hated herself. And she had no doubt at all that he hated her thoroughly. Outside their secret, wordless passion, he did everything he could to avoid her.

Which was why she was astounded when one morning, as he had done before, he shook her awake. This time there was no casual friendliness in the gesture. His face was taut with dislike and, as soon as she had turned and opened her eyes, his hand fell away from her shoulder as if her flesh burned him.

'You will have to come with me today. We are going to

Augusto's stronghold.' And, as she stared at him, impatiently, 'Don't look like that! I've told Miguel to come too. So you'll have someone to *talk* to.' His tone bit.

Julia flushed miserably. Roberto surveyed her unsmilingly for a second before turning on his booted heel and striding out. No threats this time to dress her himself if she were tardy. Nevertheless she scrambled into her clothes as though the devil were after her.

It was a hard ride and he took it at a punishing pace. Once or twice Miguel protested, but Julia, always last of the three, said nothing. They reached the little village— for it was no more than that—in three hours.

As they rode into it, down the windy, uneven track that imperceptibly became a cobbled thoroughfare, Olivados narrowed his eyes.

'There are too many people here. Has Augusto betrayed us?'

'Augusto,' said Roberto with satisfaction, 'is on the other side of the mountain where he thinks I am in secret conference with President Valetta.'

'Oh.' Miguel stood in his stirrups scanning the street ahead of them. 'There are still a lot of people here.'

'So there should be. It is Conchita Lebecque's wedding day.'

'Oh.' Miguel sat down again slowly, casting Roberto a look of some respect. 'You planned this.'

'Let us just say I thought it time Julia saw one of our typical festivals,' Roberto said blandly. He did not look at Julia.

'Naturally.' Miguel was dry. 'And of course old Lebecque was happy to invite you, you both being lawyers, after all.'

'Precisely.'

They rode into the little street and Julia realised that, in thinking it was just a village, she had been mistaken. The road down which they were approaching it was unimpressive enough, but it opened out into a wider boulevard, set with precision-planted palm trees that led in its turn to an impressive square. The road surface was still dust and pebbles, and the pavement no better, but at least there were vehicles here as well as horses and donkeys, and a large, hurrying crowd, most of whom ignored the three.

'Where are we going? The bride's house?' asked Miguel.

Roberto shook his head. 'No, we will go to the inn. Lebecque promised me that his wife would find some festive costumes for us. We must not look out of place among the wedding guests.'

'Are you trying to look inconspicuous?' Miguel gave a crack of laughter. 'When you must have just about the best known face in the country apart from one or two military gentlemen!'

'You exaggerate,' Roberto looked faintly annoyed.

'No, I don't—and you know I don't. You shouldn't go squiring international cabaret stars if you don't want to get your picture in the papers,' Miguel insisted irrepressibly.

'You are ridiculous!' snapped Roberto, with a look of irritation at both of them. He spurred on to the inn in evident disgust.

Miguel laughed. 'The tiger does not like to be twitched by the tail,' he said obscurely in answer to Julia's raised eyebrows. 'And how unusually touchy he is becoming!' He primmed his mouth and shook his head in mock sorrow, though his eyes danced.

Julia judged it best not to get involved. She returned a noncommittal answer and, as soon as they arrived at the small inn, asked to go to the room that had been prepared for her. Of Roberto there was no sign. What there was, however, laid out on the bed, was a beautiful embroidered skirt, worked in silver and gold thread on black cloth, with a full-sleeved blouse and a black bolero. She looked at it blankly.

'You are supposed to put it on,' said a voice behind her.

She turned. Roberto stood in the doorway, attired in black high-waisted trousers and a full-sleeved shirt whose embroidery was every bit as elaborate. He was freshly shaven, his dark hair combed back sleekly from his forehead as if he was fresh from the shower, too. He looked so handsome that her mouth went dry and she stood and stared at him, incapable of speech.

'It is standard wedding guest garb,' he prompted, sounding amused. She had thought she would never hear that note of suppressed laughter again; he had been so cold, so polite, when he spoke to her these last days.

Foolishly, her eyes pricked with tears. He saw it at once and came forward. With one gentle finger he received a gathered teardrop and held it for her to see gravely.

'It is nothing to cry about.'

Julia lifted drowned eyes to his face. 'But I'm here under false pretences.'

He swore softly. 'You are here as my lady. You have every right to be here.'

'Not if they knew the truth about me.'

He looked down at her, his eyes brilliant. 'I think they know the truth better than you do,' he said enigmatically. 'Now get dressed, I promise you'll enjoy yourself.'

To her amazement, she found he was right. For one thing, he never left her side. For another, the wedding was quite a sophisticated affair, with separate ceremonies in the church and the town hall, and an enormous open air party in the square afterwards. Julia was so busy looking around at all this strangeness that she had no time to remember her problems.

Roberto, having ignored her for days, was putting himself out to see that she enjoyed herself. She realised that. Eventually, after two glasses of some pungent fruit concoction and an energetic folk dance with Miguel, she plucked up courage to ask him why.

He shrugged. 'Oh, I enjoy weddings. I would like you to enjoy them too.'

She remembered that Marta had said he had agreed with his mother that he must marry when the campaign was over. Her stomach felt hollow, but she said brightly, 'I hear you'll be having your own wedding in the not too distant future,' hating herself for the archness of it, and unable to restrain her painful curiosity.

His mouth lifted in a wry smile. 'That depends on the lady.'

It was odd how just a few words could hurt as badly as a blow. Julia went on smiling. 'Doesn't it always?'

'Not entirely, I would say. It is not because of a lady that I have not married before, for example.'

'R-really? You mean you were a bachelor by conviction?' she asked lightly.

He laughed. 'That's one way of putting it, certainly. I'd seen rather a lot of my parents' marriage first hand, and I knew it was not for me. I know too much of the way my mother operates to retain any illusions about the fair sex.'

'So what made you change your mind?'

Roberto's shoulders lifted in his characteristic, devastating shrug. 'The lady, of course. What else?'

'What indeed?' Her smile felt pasted on with her lipstick, rigid and painful.

'One look and I was lost.' He laughed ruefully, affectionately. What would it be like to have Roberto in love with you? 'One reads about it and can never imagine it happening and then, suddenly, there it is.'

Julia swallowed. 'I congratulate you,' she said through stiff lips.

He leaned forward, his eyes warm and friendly for once. She could not bear the friendliness, not when she knew he was lost to her. She made an instinctive gesture of repudiation, which she did not realise she had made, until the warmth died out of his face and he drew back.

'Don't you believe in love?' he asked coolly, apparently amused. In her turn, Julia shrugged in answer.

'Never been in love, Julia?' he pursued softly.

Never been in love! This was unendurable. She looked away.

'Define your terms,' she said with an effort.

For a moment he looked almost angry, then he laughed. 'Yes, you're not exactly a romantic, are you? A man could break up trying to persuade you to love him.'

She swallowed. 'It depends what you mean by love.'

'Oh,' he considered it, head tilted, 'wanting to see the beloved happy, perhaps. Wanting to *make* her happy. Wanting her good before your own, because if she is hurt, you are hurt, and much worse than if you are hurt in your own person.' He paused. 'Does that make sense?'

Julia was shaken. 'Yes.'

Another, longer pause, then he said quietly, 'Is that what you felt for this—Hugh?'

She jumped. 'What do you mean?'

'That was the name you called me when I roused you from sleep—Hugh. Is he your lover?'

'I have no lover,' Julia told him without expression.

His eyes narrowed. 'Hugh?'

Her mouth twisted a little. 'Hugh was ten years ago, when I was naïve and intense and still believed in that love you were talking about. He didn't.'

Roberto was watching her, studying her almost as if she were a subject on which he was experimenting. Julia shifted.

'He hurt you.' It was a statement.

'Then? Yes,' she agreed honestly. 'Not any more. It was a useful education in its way.'

'Education for what? Who has there been since?'

She did not ask him what business it was of his. She felt strangely fatalistic, as if they had been moving towards this conversation ever since they met. 'Nobody.'

'*What?*' It was almost voiceless. For some reason she could not guess at, he looked shocked.

'Nobody since Hugh,' she repeated.

'In ten years you have let no other man get close to you?' He sounded appalled.

'It's not so strange. I've always been a solitary. There'd never been anyone before Hugh that I thought I was close to: not in my family, not in my immediate circle. When I found Hugh was an illusion, I realised that I was not meant for—intimacy.' She sighed. 'Some people aren't, I think. I have friends, good friends; but I'm not the most important person in anybody's world, and that's what I want. Can you understand that?'

'Very easily,' he said in a constrained tone. 'There was a time when I felt something of that myself. But that was because my family were pushing in too close, not because they were too remote. But I understand that it is liberating to be one on your own, responsible to and for no one.'

Julia sighed. 'Yes.'

'Only it did not make me happy,' Roberto went on. He looked at her curiously. 'Are you happy?'

She tried to lighten the mood. 'Well, obviously not at the moment, I shouldn't think anyone is wild about being kidnapped.'

It might have been a trick of the light, but she thought then, just for a second, that his face whitened as if he had been mortally hurt. But no, it must have been her imagination. He was still lounging in his chair, playing idly with the glass on the table in front of him, looking amused.

'In general I'm happy enough,' Julia finished in a subdued voice.

She thought he would have said more, but at that moment they were interrupted by the wedding party. The bride, a plump, pretty girl in embroidered dress and veil, had been flinging her arms exuberantly round all the guests as they wished her well. Roberto, however, awed her into shyness. She lowered her eyes and blushed as he stood up to greet her and, bending, kissed her cheek. Her father looked gratified.

'Señor Don Roberto, we are honoured—deeply honoured. May I introduce my new son-in-law?'

The two men bowed, exchanging greetings. Somewhere among the accompanying press of friends and relations a flash camera flared. Roberto looked rueful.

'I'm sorry, my friend, I seem to have brought the newspapers with me.'

Señor Lebecque made a large gesture. 'It does not matter. They were here anyway for the civic reception tonight. When they heard you were at my little Conchita's wedding they could not keep away.' He suddenly gave a wide grin. 'It means there will be some wonderful professional wedding photographs for which I will not get a bill!'

Roberto laughed. 'Quite a consolation, that!'

Lebecque gave a mock groan. 'It is not to be underrated. Thank God I have only one daughter. You have no idea what weddings cost, Don Roberto.' He chuckled. 'Though they tell me you'll be finding out soon enough!'

Roberto stayed calm. 'Yes, I have too many sisters to be let off scot free, that is true,' he said blandly. 'But you remind me that I have not introduced you. Julia, this is Paul Lebecque, a foreigner like yourself for many years, though I suppose presiding over a local wedding now makes him a native. Paul, my companion, Doña Julia Lennox from New York.'

'A very great privilege, Doña Julia,' he said formally, adding with slightly less formality, 'I see they did not lie when they told me your eyes were the colour of the morning sky.'

Julia was startled and slightly uncomfortable. For one thing she was not used to receiving flowery compliments. For another, she could not imagine who could have talked to Lebecque about her. Unless, perhaps, Miguel

Olivados had come across him today and mentioned her.

'Thank you,' she said with some constraint.

'You are very welcome, *señorita*. I hope you will be very happy with us,' Paul Lebecque told her with a little bow.

Before she could answer, his whole party moved on to the next table and he, perforce, was carried along with it. Julia stared after him, concerned, then turned worried eyes on Roberto.

'He spoke as if I'm going to stay in this country for ever. Have you told me the truth?' Her voice rose in anxiety. 'Is there something I don't know?'

'Yes,' said Roberto lazily. 'And yes.'

She could have stamped her foot. 'What do you mean?'

'Think about it,' he advised. 'It is not so very difficult.' His mouth quirked and he imitated the tone she used when she had told him to define what he meant by love. 'And you have all the relevant information.'

She shivered. 'I don't know what you intend to do with me.'

'No,' he agreed thoughtfully. 'I should have told you that tonight is going to be rather more formal than you have become accustomed to in our country.'

'Tonight? More wedding festivities?'

'No,' he said, sitting down again, scanning the crowd. 'No, much more boring. It is an annual ritual, the businessmen of the town and countryside have a reception to which they invite people they think important. Tonight they have the Finance Minister among others.'

'And you?'

'And us,' he corrected.

'And Augusto?'

He looked surprised, then laughed. 'No. Augusto runs this town from the vantage point of organised crime. He takes his cut, he pulls strings behind the scenes, but he is not invited to meet the Minister of Finance. He would not want to be.'

Julia surveyed him. 'So why was it so important to get Augusto out of the way before you came here?'

'We came here,' he reminded her, smiling. 'Well, Augusto may be indifferent to the Minister of Finance, who offers him no threat. But I am different. He sees me as a rival. He does not know I have been invited, though he vetted the guest list weeks ago. Some of the local businessmen have had the courage to try to make a move without Augusto. By the time he finds out it will be too late—or so I hope.'

She said slowly, 'Things are coming to a head, aren't they?'

He did not answer.

'You have got your secret meeting with the President arranged? And then you will take over the country, you and your associates.'

'No,' he said, shaking his head. 'No, then there will be elections. The interim government will last six weeks at the most. I do not,' he mimicked her, '*take over* things.'

Julia forbore to say that he had taken over herself very completely. She said, 'Tonight is very important, isn't it?'

'Yes,' Roberto agreed. 'In a number of ways. And you will be very important too. You must realise that you are here as my—er—official companion. Can I rely on you not to let me down?'

Julia considered that for a long moment. To pretend, for one evening, that they belonged together, even that she was his wife: could she do it? How badly would it hurt? But he was waiting for an answer, and of course there was only one thing to say.

'I shall do my best not to burst into song after the second glass of champagne,' she assured him.

He laughed and put a hand over her own where it lay on the table.

'Thank you—though it seems a pity. We will have the songs and champagne on another occasion, I promise.'

And he raised her hand to his lips and kissed her fingers lightly.

That evening was a revelation to Julia. She had seen Roberto in formal evening clothes before, in the nightclub in Alto Rio, but she had never seen him look so impressive. Clearly his evening clothes had been delivered to the small hotel during the afternoon, as had her own.

Or rather, she thought wryly, taking several hundred dollars' worth of couture silk out of its tissue wrapping, the dress that had been provided for her to wear. It was very simply cut, with a halter neck and deeply banded waist, printed in charcoal and sapphire. She wondered who had lent it to her and whether she had done so willingly.

Before they left for the reception, Roberto came to her room with a flat leather case in his hand. Julia was standing in front of the mirror, twisting her hair so that it framed her face in soft waves before being caught up in a chignon. For a moment he stood looking at her in silence.

'Yes,' he said thoughtfully. 'Earrings. I should have thought of that.'

She turned, jumping. He strolled forward and turned her back to face the mirror. Then he extracted from its case a diamond collar with a magnificent rose diamond drop suspended from it and slid it round her throat. She gasped, at the coldness of the stone, the warmth of his hands, the whole unexpected magnificence of it.

'The family jewels,' he murmured. 'Well, one of them. No, don't take it off. It will be expected.'

Julia had not understood him, but she had acquiesced. It was only later, as she trod solemnly beside him in the procession to the High Table under a barrage of photographers' cameras and television lights, that she realised exactly how public an occasion it was.

And throughout the evening it became more and more evident that Roberto was an important figure. His speech was short but listened to more attentively than any of the others. He was pursued by the reporters. All his fellow guests were anxious to have words with him. And, in his reflected glory, Julia found herself treated like a queen.

The women were friendly but profoundly respectful, the men overwhelming. She was congratulated on her dress, her hair, her command of Spanish and, of course, Roberto. She began to feel like his consort.

And he, for all that he was so much in demand, was attentive and considerate, as if she were something precious which had to be protected from the buffeting of so many interested people. He hardly left her side. He held her hand, put his arm round her shoulders, kissed her fingertips countless times throughout the evening. Once, when a wisp of hair began to droop from her chignon, he pinned it back for her, using the small service as an excuse to trail his fingers across her cheek and dropping a swift kiss on her temple.

It was exquisitely done. To anybody watching it must have looked as if he could not keep his hands off her, Julia thought, aching. It almost looked like that to her. If she had not known that he regarded the pretence as an insurance policy for her safety—if he had not told her himself that he was hoping to marry a lady with whom he had found himself in love—she could have been wooed so easily into believing it was real. She dreaded the thought of him coming to her room that night. She did not think she would be able to contain her hurt and grief.

In the hotel lobby she turned to him, driven by fear. 'Please,' she said in a shaking voice from which all her social poise had been shockingly banished, 'please let me be alone tonight. I—need to think.'

'Think?' He sounded amused but he looked down at her gravely. 'Are you sure that's what you want?'

She nodded, unable to speak. He gave a great sigh then and kissed her gently on the forehead before turning away without a word.

The next day he sent her home with Miguel. He did not return for two nights and when he did he was taciturn to the point of rudeness. Her respite was over: he made love to her with a ruthless thoroughness that said, more clearly than words, that he despised her and himself for their mutual passion.

Julia felt she would never be whole again. Roberto had somehow chemically made himself part of her so that, even without love, she was committed to him for ever.

And she wondered how long it would be before he found out that commitment. It would be the end of any last hope she had of getting away once he did. He was adept at eliciting her feelings, no matter how hard she strove to suppress them, and then turning them as weapons against her.

She did her best to avoid him by day, and she thought Roberto did the same. It was therefore a surprise and a dismay to her when one day he had not left the little house. Normally he had gone long before she awoke.

She turned on her side, aching from last night and slightly muzzy-headed, when he said from behind her, 'I shall be teaching several of the women to use hand guns this morning. When you are dressed we can go.'

Julia sat up at once, pushing an unsteady hand through her hair. The sheet fell away from her, but she made no attempt to retrieve it. She had gone far beyond modesty now; Roberto knew each nerve and pulse and every responsive inch of her body. There was nothing worth hiding from him except her feelings.

She said blankly, 'Hand guns?'

'It could be necessary.' Roberto was glacial. He flicked a look at his watch. 'You have slept late. Be outside in ten minutes.' He looked up and the slatey eyes locked with hers. 'Or,' he said softly, 'I will come and get you whether you are dressed or not.'

He went out before she could answer, but she would not have argued. She believed him; she had learned that Roberto never threatened anything he was not prepared to put into practice. The lesson, she thought wryly, had cost her her self-respect, and she was not likely to forget it.

She was outside in the sun, blinking, within the ten minutes he had set. She saw him at once. He and Marta were with a group of the village women outside Angelina's house. Julia went towards them reluctantly.

Marta greeted her warmly, but Roberto ignored her. He was folding the gnarled hand of Angelina's sister-in-law round a small shiny black object and giving her gentle-voiced instruction. Julia shivered. The gun filled her with horror, like an evil taste in the mouth.

She said nothing, though, sitting quietly on the steps of Angelina's wooden verandah, while Marta and Roberto encouraged the elderly woman. At length they finished with her, not, by the look of it, very successfully. Roberto turned to Julia.

'Your turn,' he said briefly. 'Give me your hand.'

Oddly, since he had touched and tasted and moulded every limb of her body, Julia was shy. A faint flush rose in her cheeks as she reluctantly extended her right hand. He put the dark thing into it. The gun was still warm from the old woman's hand. It felt like a heavy, deadly slug.

Julia's mouth twisted in ungovernable distaste. 'I can't,' she protested, trying to repudiate it, to give it back to him.

His brows twitched together in a formidable frown.

'For God's sake don't start getting temperamental,' he said in English before he switched back to his own language to instruct her.

She stared down at the thing, at his fingers twining round her own, showing her how to balance, how to turn it, how to point . . .

'I can't!' she repeated, wrenching her hand away from
him.

'Don't be a fool!' This time Roberto spoke in Spanish.
'The whole country is mobilised. You have to—for your
own protection and the good of us all.'

Julia stared down at the little engine in her hands. It
was snub-nosed, ugly. Roberto was so close, she could so
easily point the thing at him, watch the bullet rip into his
flesh, see him die. She could not, she *could* not do that to
anyone. The thought of Roberto bleeding, falling, his
eyes clouding like a wounded animal's, was more than
she could bear. She threw the gun down hard and the dust
spurted as it fell. Roberto lunged forward, his mouth a
thin line.

'You criminal fool! You didn't even know whether it
was loaded!'

'I can't!' Julia's voice rose hysterically. 'The very
thought of it makes me sick—I can't do it!'

Roberto took her wrist in an iron grip, forcing her arm
down so that her knees buckled.

'Pick it up.' He was implacable.

Her wrist was on fire. 'No. I won't shoot guns!'

'Pick—it—up!'

He had forced her on to her knees now, and the little
gritty stones grazed her as she knelt in the dust. She
shook her head. A small sob escaped her.

'Hurting people, killing people—that's all you understand!' She shook her hair back, glaring up at him,
suddenly brave in her defiance. 'Well, I'm not going to
add to it. I don't care what you do to me, I am not going to
touch that thing!'

She might just as well not have spoken.

'Pick it up.'

Their eyes locked. 'Never,' said Julia with the absolute
calm of despair. She shut her eyes briefly to close out his
expression of furious contempt. 'It disgusts me.' She

risked opening her eyes again. Against the brilliant
morning sky his figure was coming and going oddly, but
she could see that his face was white beneath the tan—
presumably with anger, because she had again publicly
denied his domination over her. '*You* disgust me,' she
said with precision, before the pain in her wrists became
blinding and, to her great surprise, she toppled sideways
into oblivion.

There was a great roaring in her ears. She was in a
crowded New York street and had fallen and was being
trodden underfoot. Or no, she was being kicked like a
football. She hurt and she was powerless and all the world
was shouting at her.

She gave a small sob of protest and was instantly
startled by cool fingers on her forehead.

'Be still,' said Roberto in a voice she did not recognise
from him.

Her lashes fluttered, lifted, fluttered down again and
then, like a thunderbolt, she was in full possession of the
whole of that ugly scene again. She came fully awake.

She was on a bed, not the one in what she had come to
regard as her own house. Angelina was hovering in the
background, but all Julia could see, what filled her
vision, was Roberto, very tall and straight, beside the
bed.

His fingers lifted. He looked strange, she thought.

'You are recovered?'

Behind him Angelina murmured something. His lips
compressed and a muscle moved in his cheek.

'Do you feel—' he hesitated, 'ill?'

Julia put a hand to her head, pressing it slightly against
her brows.

'I feel odd,' she admitted in a puzzled voice. 'I'm
sorry—I didn't realise I felt so strongly.'

For a moment his brows twitched together, then he
said, 'Oh, about the revolver. Forget it. It does not
matter.'

Julia stared at him. If it did not matter, why had he gone to such lengths to make her obey him? Was it just his pride, his determination to subjugate her? Her eyes filled with pain. He made a move as if he would lean forward and touch her. She flinched. At once he drew back.

'You must stay here with Angelina,' he said with constraint, 'until you are recovered.' He paused as if waiting for her to speak.

Julia said nothing. She did not know what he wanted from her and her head had begun to pound sickeningly. It must be the altitude, she thought. She had escaped altitude sickness for so long that she had thought she was immune, but clearly she had been wrong.

'Very well.'

Still he did not go. 'Do you want anything?'

My freedom, thought Julia wryly, knowing even as the thought came to her that it was not wholly true. Though she did want peace, an uninterrupted sleep even.

She sighed. 'Just to be alone.'

Roberto did not say anything. When she looked, he had gone.

CHAPTER EIGHT

JULIA slept for most of the rest of the morning. Once or twice she was aware of Angelina but she did not really wake up properly until she heard the clink of pottery.

'You will be better,' said Angelina firmly in her ear, 'for a hot drink.'

Julia opened her eyes slowly and smiled at the older woman. She pulled herself up on to an elbow and held out her hand for the mug.

'I'm sure I will,' she agreed, still a trifle sleepily. 'What is it?'

Angelina told her, watching with satisfaction as she sipped at it.

'It's good,' said Julia, trying not to sound surprised. 'Is it a traditionl remedy for altitude sickness?'

Angelina looked at her for a moment. 'We use it for a lot of things,' she said at last. 'It is strengthening.'

'It is indeed.' Julia drained the mug and set it down carefully, then gave herself a little shake. 'I feel quite different.'

'Well enough to get up?'

'Oh, certainly.' Julia swung her legs off the bed to prove it and stood up. There was no hint of that light-headedness or the faint nausea she had felt before. 'Back on track,' she told Angelina cheerfully.

Her companion looked alarmed. 'You are not well enough to go scrambling around in the high fields again,' she said, obviously reporting verbatim what had been said to her. Her next words confirmed it. 'Don Roberto says so.'

Julia frowned. 'Don Roberto is an expert on altitude sickness?'

For a moment Angelina seemed to hesitate, then she shrugged.

'In the circumstances, does he not have a right to advise you, *señorita*?'

'A right to order me around, you mean,' said Julia discontentedly. They were all the same in this village: Don Roberto's word was law, whether he was being reasonable or not! She had no hope of being allowed to disobey him. 'Oh, very well. There's nothing I can do about it, I suppose.'

Angelina surveyed her with a certain amount of sympathy. 'Believe me, it will be better for you to stay here with us. They say Augusto is in the hills, although he told the others that he would go south. He does not trust Don Roberto, I think.'

Remembering the little piggy eyes and the bandit's silent spying on Roberto and herself, Julia shivered.

'All right, you've convinced me,' she allowed, giving Angelina a rueful smile. 'Only what shall I do with myself?'

The other returned her smile, appearing relieved. 'There will be no problem. My sister-in-law and I will teach you to weave,' she said kindly, as if Julia were a sulky six-year-old complaining of boredom.

Which, thought Julia, chastened, was not so far from the truth. She thanked Angelina in a subdued voice and allowed herself to be escorted to another smaller house and was introduced to its friendly occupant and the handloom she wielded. In the end, she grew fascinated and spent an absorbed day trying her hand at weaving the heavy llama wool under the enthusiastic guidance of her mentor. When the heat of the day was over they took the work outside and when darkness fell, with its habitual suddenness, stopped and went to Angelina's house.

For once there was no sign of Roberto at Angelina's hospitable table. Julia hesitated to ask where he was. It was clear that her companions were all serenely convinced that she knew as much if not more than they did. This impression was not dispelled by Roberto's eventual arrival very late. He came straight to her, took her hand and bent and kissed her lips proprietorially.

'You're looking better. Good,' he said, before seating himself on the bench beside her where one of the young men made room for him. Angelina brought him a plate of stew and he thanked her with a smile. 'I was worried.'

Against her will, almost, Julia was touched. He might not be in love with her, he might have used her very badly, but nevertheless, in spite of all his cares and dangerous activities, he found time to concern himself over her slight indisposition.

'It was nothing,' she assured him. 'Soon over.'

'Yes?' Roberto sounded sceptical. 'Not that there is very much I can do about it at the moment, though I hope that will change in the next few days.'

Julia looked at him sharply. Their companions were talking as usual, volubly and loudly. She switched into English.

'Do you mean that the fighting is over?'

Roberto looked at his plate, his mouth grim. 'It soon will be, one way or another. And provided the bandit doesn't decide to stir things up.'

She said, 'How long?'

He cast her a quick unsmiling look. 'Are you so anxious to get away?'

'Naturally,' she said as coolly as she could, though her heart started beating hard at something she thought she saw in his eyes.

He looked away again, sighing. 'Yes, I suppose so. I'm sorry. As for how long—well, it could be this week, if we are lucky. We are already negotiating. The trouble is the Air Force on their side and the bandit on ours. Both may have decided to seize the opportunity to make a bid for all-out power.' He smiled bitterly. 'Not helped by the fact that Pepe has allowed the Air Force to identify the radio lorry. I only hope he has the good sense to keep it off the road and stop broadcasting. It could be very dangerous if he takes it to a village where the Air Force can spot it.'

'Why?' asked Julia, puzzled.

'They don't just have aeroplanes and gold braid, you know,' Roberto said ironically. 'They have guns and bombs as well. They could wipe out any village where they found that truck. And they would do it too.'

Julia swallowed. 'I see.'

'I thought you would. Especially given your views on firearms.'

She winced at the dry tone. 'I—I've already apologised for that.'

'So you have.' He looked down at her enigmatically. 'Are you expecting an apology from me in my turn?'

Julia returned his look steadily. 'I am due one, I think.'

'You've said that to me before.' His voice was very low. 'Why do you fight me all the time, Julia?'

Her eyes widened. The air in the crowded, friendly house was suddenly stifling. She put a hand to her throat.

'You know why,' she said in a strangled voice.

'Do I? Sometimes I wonder.'

'Nobody likes being kidnapped,' she said distantly. 'And caged, and bullied. And—and *manipulated*,' she finished in a rush.

Roberto laughed aloud at that, throwing his head back. 'Is that what you call it? How very unromantic!'

She glared at him. He met her look with a quizzical smile and flicked her nose with his thumb. Then, quite unconcerned, he finished his meal, exchanging a few words with his other neighbour and the people opposite him.

As soon as he had finished he swung his leg back over the bench and stood up, drawing her after him. Several heads turned. There was a murmur of goodnights, a cheerful wave from Angelina at her cooking pots, and they left. Once inside their own house, Roberto swung her round to face him, as he leaned negligently back against the door. In the dark she could not make out his expression but she knew from his hands and his voice that he was laughing.

'Nobody likes being what?' he murmured.

For the first time in days, Julia tried to escape.

'Let me alone,' she said, pulling away fruitlessly.

'Not on your life,' he said, chuckling. 'Not for a moment. Not until we've proved that some people,' he was speaking between little kisses, placed delicately on her sensitised skin, 'don't—mind—at—all.'

Julia gave up. He was stronger than she was, anyway, she told herself. There was no point in fighting the two of them, Roberto and her treacherous, acquiescent, hungry body. She went into his arms, as she always did.

That night, though, and the nights that followed, were different. The passion was still there for both of them but Roberto seemed gentler, sometimes even tentative, as if he was waiting for a sign or a word from her. Julia was bewildered but too shy to ask him, in the light of day, what it was that he was seeking. And at night, of course, they did not talk.

By day, too, she was still oddly fragile. Hints of the dizziness recurred. Even without his prohibition she did not think she would have gone far from the village; her legs felt too shaky and she seemed drained of energy. Once or twice she caught Roberto looking at her narrowly, as if he suspected that she was far from well. But he had already got enough to worry about, she reasoned, so when he asked her point blank how she felt she denied all weakness. His mouth tightened and she did not think he believed her. But he did not press the point.

He was clearly very busy. Sometimes he disappeared for hours. Twice he was gone overnight, returning in the morning heavy-eyed and unshaven. He did not tell Julia what he was doing and she, fearful, did not ask. The village, however, became noticeably busier with people arriving at all hours of the day and night. Julia concentrated on her weaving lessons and kept herself out of the bustle.

It was there, weaving in the sunshine, that Miguel Olivados found her one morning as he strolled past.

'You're looking more and more domesticated,' he greeted her, leaning on the verandah rail and smiling down at her.

Julia looked up with a chuckle. 'Do you realise that back home in New York people would pay hundreds, if not thousands, of dollars for these lessons that I'm getting free?'

'I can imagine. And are you a good pupil?'

'They tell me I'm a natural,' Julia said with pride. 'It's very comforting' she added candidly, 'as I've always been hopeless at knitting and sewing and things. Now I shall be able to squash all my handicraft-mad friends by showing them my own weaving.'

Miguel's eyes danced. 'Definitely superior!'

'Oh quite. So these last weeks will at least have that to show for themselves.'

Miguel looked at her curiously. 'And is that all? Just weaving?'

Julia lifted one shoulder. 'I suppose my Spanish has improved, as well.'

He looked faintly worried. Clasping his hands round his elbows he leant forward. 'And Roberto?'

There was a little silence, while Julia willed herself not to blush. She let her eyes slide past him and said in a brittle, sophisticated voice, 'Oh, he hasn't improved at all. He's the same arrogant bully he was when his henchmen first kidnapped me.'

Olivados was silent. Then he said quietly, 'Doña Julia, I have told you before—it is very unfair to Roberto to blame him for circumstances which are not of his making.'

She gave a harsh laugh. 'And you think the circumstances in which I find myself are *not* of his making?'

To her surprise he looked faintly embarrassed. 'Now, I can see that that is different. But earlier—he was in a very difficult position. He did what he could to see that you were safe,' he added, not very clearly, Julia thought.

'Well he has had a major achievement then, because I am still safe. And I shall even *feel* safe when I get home and put all this behind me.'

For a long moment he looked at her. Then he said, 'You sound so bitter.'

Julia looked down at her work. 'Do I?'

'You have been so unhappy with us?' he probed. 'We have hurt you? Neglected you?'

'You have all been very kind,' she said woodenly.

'Then what——' He stopped dead. 'Roberto,' he said at last, not much above a whisper. 'It is he who has hurt you.'

Julia did not answer. She bent over her weaving again, her face expressionless.

'But I could have sworn——' Again Miguel broke off. He looked down compassionately at her bent head. He said, 'If it is Florita who worries you, Doña Julia, you can put her out of your head. They meet only because of the campaign.'

Julia did not say that she had not known that Roberto had been meeting Florita at all, but she flinched. Miguel looked even more anxious.

He said urgently, 'Truly, you must believe me. All that was over long ago when Florita decided she wanted her career. I have known Roberto all my life, and I can vouch for it. She is no threat to you.' He added, not very reassuringly to Julia's way of thinking, 'She would never marry him.'

Threading a strand of chestnut wool with great care,

Julia said evenly, 'Whether she would or would not, it's nothing to do with me. And I don't want to hear about it.'

She looked up then and met his eyes. He straightened at once and took a step back, making her a little bow.

'Of course. Forgive me.'

They talked a little more, in rather strained commonplaces, and then Miguel left. But Roberto must have heard about it because he said to her that night before dinner. 'You have seen Miguel?'

Julia stared at him. 'What of it?'

'What did he say?'

She flushed faintly. Had he primed Miguel and if so why? She could not imagine but she was not going to admit to him that she and Miguel had been discussing him. She lifted her chin.

'Nothing.'

Roberto gave her a hard stare. 'You talked for twenty minutes about nothing?'

'What an excellent spy system you have,' she said in congratulatory tones. 'Was it really twenty minutes? I wasn't timing it myself.'

He swore virulently. 'Sometimes I could beat you.'

'I wonder if I'd notice any difference,' said Julia, very nastily, because for some unaccountable reason she was near to tears at his harshness.

He gave her one look of loathing and slammed out of the house without replying. He was gone three days.

This time it was clear not only that the villagers knew where Roberto had gone but also that they were under orders not to tell Julia. She tried not to consider the possibility that he was at another of these essential tactical meetings with Florita, but she could not quite banish the possibility from her mind. As a result she was racked with a bitter pain which she reluctantly at last diagnosed as jealousy. She wondered if it was as obvious to other people as it was to herself. When she asked Miguel Olivados outright where Roberto was, he only looked uncomfomfortable and answered at random. She did not try again.

It was with mixed feelings therefore that one night, late, when she was unwillingly thinking of going to bed, she was startled out of her reverie by a thumping crash. She jumped up, turning. The door had been flung back on its hinges and in the doorway stood Roberto. He was swaying.

Julia's first thought was that he was hurt. He looked ghastly, his face grey and covered with dust, his eyes bloodshot. In pure instinct she ran to him and put steadying arms round him. He crushed her against him and she found he was shaking.

'Hold me,' he said in a voice she did not recognise.

They stood in a convulsive embrace for several seconds. Then, as the cold of the night surged in, Julia said gently, 'We must close the door. Come inside.'

Half dazedly, Roberto did so, not letting go of her, though his frenzied grip relaxed slightly.

She said in a careful voice, 'Are you hurt?'

'Me?' He sounded blank. 'No. Though it was close. God knows what might have happened.'

Julia's heart began to slam hard against her ribs. She recognised alarm. But refusing to let it show, she asked steadily, 'What was close, Roberto?'

He hugged her again, hard, not answering.

'Tell me!'

'Those boys,' he said into her hair. 'Those stupid, stupid boys.'

'Pepe's friends?'

He nodded and passed a weary hand over his face. He was looking drained. Julia pushed him gently towards the bed and, when he sat down, sank to her knees beside him, still with her arms round him.

'What happened?' she asked him calmly.

Roberto looked down at her, and she could see lingering horror in the eyes which were no longer slatey cool but molten with feeling. He pushed fingers which shook slightly through his tumbled hair.

'They'd been drinking. And they've been seeing a lot of Augusto—I didn't know about that. We went to a meeting—did I tell you?'

She shook her head, not interrupting.

'Oh no, I remember, I thought . . .' He broke off. 'Well, anyway, we arranged a meeting to negotiate with the old government. It was supposed to be secret. And secure.' He gave a harsh laugh. 'Pepe brought the radio truck which the Air Force have been following for a week. He might just as well have hung up a neon sign.'

Julia was filled with horror. 'Did they—shoot?'

He shook his head, 'No, the planes were too high. They obviously didn't have any bombs on board or we'd all be dead. And those stupid boys *laughed*! They were like children.'

She took his hands and held them between her own.

'And then Pepe brought out a hand-grenade—said Valetta should sign unconditional surrender or he'd blow us all up. Said he'd be proud to die for his country.' Roberto sounded despairing. 'Of course the soldiers all started fingering their weapons but Pepe was waving the grenade around and they couldn't do a thing.'

Julia was very white. 'What did you do?' she asked, not doubting that it was Roberto who had resolved the situation.

'I jumped Pepe.' It was said with a kind of blank weariness that was somehow more terrifying than his anger.

She swallowed. 'Did you kill him?'

'I thought I was going to have to.' He shut his eyes briefly. 'But in the end I got the thing away from him and ran with it. I hurled it as hard as I could into the river before it exploded. The Air Force will have seen that, too, of course.' He shrugged. 'But it couldn't be helped. After that we all left—ran like hell, to tell the truth.'

'And Pepe?'

'No, he didn't run. If I'm any judge he has a broken shoulder,' Roberto said unemotionally, 'I don't know where Pepe is now.'

Julia shuddered. 'But you're all right. Nobody was hurt,' she said, trying to encourage him.

He shrugged. 'And nothing was agreed. The soldiers won't meet me again because they won't trust my word, and who shall blame them? And the Air Force will no doubt start bombing the towns trying to flush out revolutionaries. The whole *bloody* mess will start all over again, because of an ambitious bandit and a couple of vainglorious schoolboys!'

He sounded so empty Julia could have wept. Bending so that he could not see her expression, she said, 'It may not be so bad—you can't tell yet. In the meantime you're too tired to think clearly. Let me take your boots off, and then try to get some rest.'

Automatically, it seemed, he raised first one foot and then the other. The boots were crusted with grey mud. Julia set them carefully to one side.

'Lie down,' she said softly.

With a long sigh he did so, tipping his hands behind his head. She stood up and looked down at him.

'Would you like some food? A drink?'

He shook his head, watching her. She touched his cheek fleetingly. 'Then sleep, I won't disturb you.'

The dark eyes were unwavering.

'Julia?' It was very soft, hardly above a whisper.

'Yes?'

He did not touch her, did not reach out to her. He just lay there, his hands behind his head, watching her.

'I—need you.'

She stood very still. It seemed as if the world had stopped. There was nothing in the whole world but this tiny room with its oil lamp and shifting shadows and the unfathomable gaze of the man before her. Julia did not answer, afraid of the force of her own feelings, hardly daring to breathe lest it break the spell.

As if it were wrenched out of him he said, 'Let me make love to you tonight.'

It was not, of course it was not, because he loved her. Julia faced that squarely, facing also the fact that she would have given her life to have him love her then. But he had been through a nightmare and, even though the nightmare was over, all he could see in the future was more bloodshed and pain. Tonight he sought oblivion. And she could give it to him.

Her fingers went to the collar of her shirt. With uncharacteristic clumsiness she unbuttoned it, aware that her hand was not quite steady. Her breathing was shallow and fast and—for some reason—seemed to hurt. She smiled down at him, though, withholding everything but the offer of comfort.

Roberto's eyes seemed to darken as he watched her undo and then remove her shirt. He made no move to help her. She shivered as the cold hit her naked skin and her breasts started. She looked at him steadily.

He said in a whisper, 'You're so pale. You look fragile; like seashells. Sometimes I feel I'm going to smash you.'

'No,' Julia said calmly. 'I don't break.'

She took off her jeans, briefs, socks and looked down at him, smiling crookedly. 'But I might freeze. Are you going to hold me?'

He gave a little shaken laugh and dragged her against him then. The dusty clothes were abrasive, scratching her skin, and he held her so hard that all the fastenings of his clothes bit into her.

'Gently,' she murmured. 'Or I'll have the imprints of zips all over me tomorrow!'

Roberto laughed again, holding her trapped on top of him, nuzzling her neck under the fall of dark hair.

'You're wonderful—so soft, so human. Oh God, Julia, don't fight me tonight. Give me back some peace of mind,' In spite of that laughter he sounded desperate, almost as if he were afraid. She stroked his hair tenderly. He said between his teeth, startling her, 'I will stop this bloody war if it costs me my life.'

'Don't talk like that!' At once she was tense, sharp-voiced in her fear. Then, deliberately, she steadied herself. 'Don't think like that. Think about making love to me instead.'

And, for the first time, she began to remove his clothes. After a moment he helped her, his long fingers dealing deftly with fastenings that she could not master. When he was naked she began to kiss him, slowly, as he had kissed her so many times. His chest lifted steeply in a sigh of pleasure as her mouth travelled over every vein and muscle.

In the quavery light of the oil lamp Julia could trace the perfection of his body, compact, lithe, with powerful muscles under sleek skin whose texture hurried her breath and made her fingers tremble.

'You're a voluptuary,' drawled Roberto, sounding more himself now. He was lazily amused, basking in their mutual delight with a relaxed pleasure Julia could never recall before.

'I think I must be,' she mumbled against the elegant bones of his shoulder. 'It must be your fault.'

'Excellent,' he said. 'I didn't know I had it in me.' He took over the kiss and his hands grew urgent. 'Oh Julia—Julia!'

Eventually he fell into a sleep of exhaustion. For a while she stayed awake, cradling him where he slept, his head on her breast, one arm outflung across her body. Very lightly her fingers stroked his hair from his brow. She had never felt so happy in her life, she thought, or more hopeless.

CHAPTER NINE

IN the morning Roberto was still deeply asleep. Julia edged from under him. The room smelled of oil; the lamp had burned itself out in the night. He stirred, when she wriggled out of bed, but was too profoundly unconscious to wake.

She tugged on her clothes very fast and opened the shutter a slit, just to let out the smell. It must be very early, she decided. The village street was brilliant with sunshine but deserted. She cast Roberto a doubtful look. This morning the stubble of his beard was pronounced, and involuntarily she shivered, remembering the unexpectedly erotic sensation of it against her own skin. Tenderness overwhelmed her. Whatever he felt for her, however he might have been using her, last night she had loved him and she had made him forget the horrors of the day. She would never regret it.

She had better make coffee for when he awoke, she thought, trying to be practical. The small kerosene stove was full. They often used it in the morning. She was just about to light it when she saw, to her annoyance, that they must have knocked over the water jug last night. If she was to wake him with coffee she would have to go down to the stream and fetch more water.

Taking the jug, she let herself out of the house quietly. On the bed Roberto stirred, muttered, but did not wake. Julia closed the door behind her.

The best place to collect water was just below the village, where the stream passed the little plateau on which they had parked the jeep the night they brought her here. Normally there were no vehicles there, just an odd mule or a goat or two. Today, as she rounded the corner, she saw a lorry. And, worse than that, she saw the bandit Augusto who was Roberto's enemy. He was hurrying away from the truck, downstream away from the village.

He must have heard her approach, for he suddenly turned, whipped round as if he were expecting an assassin with a knife at his back. Julia walked towards him warily, and he tipped his head back to watch her, shading his eyes.

'So,' he said, very softly, as she came up to him. 'The beautiful hostage.' He eyed her lasciviously. 'Don Roberto has all the luck. Or he has had so far.'

Julia did not ask him what he meant. She was afraid of him, but she was too level-headed to let it show. Moreover, she could see he was bursting with pride. If she showed sufficient lack of interest, she reasoned, he would tell her what had caused that air of seedy triumph. At least, that was the psychology that worked in international business meetings.

It worked now.

'He's in for a surprise,' Augusto said gloatingly. 'When he gets back this pet village of his will be flattened!'

Julia stood very still, assimilating this, trying to make sense of it. Clearly he did not know that Roberto had arrived back last night. What else did he not know? Then, with slow horror, she realised the significance of the truck. It was the one Pepe had used as a radio station. And it was parked clearly, detectably, on the outskirts of the village. What was it that Roberto had said? Pepe might as well have erected a neon sign? Well, Augusto had planted a sign, as clear as a motorway indicator, for the hunting aircraft to follow.

Her face became masklike while her brain worked

furiously. Augusto was enjoying himself, playing games with her. If he thought she really understood what he was talking about he would dispose of her without a qualm.

She said in her best little-girl voice, 'I don't understand.'

'Don't you?' He had turned, was coming back up the hillside towards her. Obviously, thought Julia in relief, he did not expect the Air Force just yet, or he would be running for his life. The keys, she saw, were still in the lorry. Presumably he did not think it worth while to remove them. That would be a help.

He was in front of her now, his breath foul in her face.

'Don't you?' he repeated. 'No, I don't suppose you do. Women only understand one thing.'

And then he pressed his mouth on hers. Julia could not suppress a sound of distaste, but she did not fight him. She stood quiescent under the onslaught, unmoved by it, until he drew back in disgust.

'By God, you must have milk in your veins, just as you look!' he spat.

She thought then that he would release her and walk away, making good his escape while he could, but his eyes slid past her and narrowed.

'Still,' he went on, more loudly, 'if you're dish fit for a gentleman like Don Roberto there must be something to you . . .' and he flung her hard to the ground and dived down on top of her as if she were a fallen soldier.

What happened next was so fast that Julia was never afterwards able to sort it out in her mind clearly. One moment she was fighting Augusto, gagging on dust and the rank smell of his sweat, the next he had been plucked bodily from her. She struggled up to see Augusto and Roberto tumbling over and over down the slope, locked in furious combat.

She put horrified hands to her cheeks and became

simultaneously aware of two sounds, the twittering of birds, disturbed by human mayhem and the distant, obscene rumble of powerful engine. Augusto had underestimated the Air Force.

Without conscious thought, Julia jumped into the cab of the lorry and started it up. She had never driven anything so cumbersome in her life, much less on rocky and winding tracks, but she sent the vehicle down the mountainside at a speed which would have appalled her had she been a passenger. It rocked wildly and all its hinges groaned, but it did not actually go over.

Before the aircraft were visible in the sky she was on the main road.

They were not bombers; they were small, light aircraft and they tried to stop the lorry by shooting at it. Julia did not know what armaments they used, but whatever they were they fell short of the truck over and over again, spraying up earth and rocks behind her and on either side of the road. In the end it was her driving and the old vehicle itself that stopped her headlong career. A sharp bend followed by an even sharper one in the opposite direction, an edge of the mountain road and too high a gear set the engine coughing, the wheels slewing, and the whole truck was sliding out of control.

The driver's door fell open. With the calm of extreme fear Julia looked down twenty vertical feet and shut her eyes as she sailed through the open door and made contact, painfully, with gorse and stones. Engine noises and the sound of fire filled her head, and she knew no more.

There was a confusion of voices. Swimming up from the depths, Julia thought she had never fainted so often or so dramatically in the whole of her life as she had done in the last few weeks. She said so but her throat was stiff and her words came out in a disjointed mumble.

A voice said in English, 'What was that, honey? Hey, you guys. I think she's conscious!'

But before she could answer she had gone dancing off down into the deeps again. At length, very slowly, she broke the surface for the last time.

She opened her eyes. It was brilliantly sunny. There were Venetian blinds casting barred shadows on the wall and on the face of the woman bending over her. The woman was dressed in crisp white cotton and looked cool. Julia did not know her.

She said, not very originally she knew, 'Where am I?'

The woman straightened. 'Good morning, Miss Lennox. How are you feeling?'

'Alive,' Julia said, trying to expel the note of faint surprise from her voice. 'Where is this? Am I in Alto Rio?'

What she was wondering, though she did not like to voice the thought, was whether she was a political prisoner as a result of her mad dash with the illegal broadcasting equipment.

The woman studied something above Julia's head, reaching out to adjust it.

'No, this is Miami,' she answered. 'This is the Havering Clinic.'

'*Miami*!' Julia jumped in amazement and felt the pull of a tube on her arm. Looking up she saw the canister above her. So she was on a saline drip. 'How the hell did I get here?'

'You were flown in two days ago,' she was told.

'But—but how? By whom?'

The nurse smiled at her. 'I'm told Technica Associates is picking up the bill. And you have a very worried boss on the line every hour!'

'Tony,' said Julia in a deflated voice. 'I see.' She bit her lip. 'What happened?'

The nurse said curiously, 'Don't you remember?'

'Not much, no,' Julia said crisply. 'Or I wouldn't be asking.'

The nurse looked slightly perturbed. 'I think you'd better see Dr Gonzalez. He'll want to know that you're conscious at last.'

She left hurriedly, and Julia sank her head back into the pillows.

They felt uncomfortably soft after the solid padding she had been sleeping on in Roberto's house. She compressed her lips against crying out. She had been brought here, shipped out, torn away from Roberto's country without knowing anything about it, and now she did not even know if he was alive or dead.

The door opened.

'Miss Lennox? I hear you're back with us.'

She opened her eyes very wide. They were glittering but tearless. She saw a short, smiling man in a white jacket with a stethoscope round his neck. He perched informally on the side of her bed, reaching almost absently for her pulse.

'As you see,' she said. And then, getting straight to the heart of what worried her, 'What happened? Was there a revolution?'

'Hey,' he joked, 'you've only just come round! I can't start talking global politics with you. It wouldn't be ethical.'

Julia drew a patient breath. 'Well, can you at least tell me what happened to me?'

'Oh, sure, I can do that.' Apparently satisfied with her pulse, he returned her wrist to her and sat back comfortably. 'You fell out of an unroadworthy heap of iron and bounced down a hillside. There was some nasty grazing, you cracked a couple of ribs and there was a head wound that bled a lot, but you'd now have to take a microscope to find the scar. You'll feel stiff for several weeks, but it's all highly repairable. In fact most of it's already being renewed by your own body right now.'

Julia surveyed him. 'So why am I here?'

'Observation,' he said promptly. 'You were unconscious.'

'Because of the blow on the head? Or because of painkillers?'

'We've had to give you a shot or two,' he admitted.

'So why else? Come on,' she said shrewdly, 'I know there's more to it than that. Tell me the bad news.'

He looked down at the backs of his hands in sudden absorption. 'To be honest, Miss Lennox, I don't know whether you'll think it bad news or not. But you'll have to know some time, I guess.' He looked up quickly. 'I'm afraid you've lost the child.'

'The *child*?' She sank back among the pillows, her face perfectly white.

Dr Gonzalez seized her wrist again, but what it told him obviously relieved his mind.

He said curiously, watching her darkening eyes, 'Did you not realise you were pregnant?'

'It never even occurred to me,' she said through cold lips. 'I didn't think about it—there was so much else wrong. I just thought it was anxiety, tension—even altitude sickness,' she said bitterly, remembering. 'I've been very stupid.'

'No, I guess you've had a bad time. The guys who brought you in told me something about it.'

Julia turned a look of painful intensity on him. 'The guys who brought me in? Who were they?'

He shrugged. 'Oh, just some people from the Consulate out there. I gather most of them were air-lifted out when the fighting started.'

'Oh,' said Julia, 'I see. Yes, of course.'

'Look,' Dr Gonzalez said carefully, 'physically you're going to come out of this in great shape—no problems. But you may have other difficulties. In a couple of days, why don't you talk to one of our counsellors? You've had a traumatic experience, and it won't be surprising if you need help. Don't be ashamed to ask for it.'

Julia closed her eyes. 'Several traumatic experiences,' she said drily. 'And the best help I can get at the moment is a long dose of my own company with no intrusions. I need to do some hard thinking, and I'd rather do it in private.'

'Sure.' He rose, quite unoffended. 'I'll tell the staff to keep out of your hair. Until they next have to come and stick a needle in you, of course. But otherwise, strict privacy. Just ring if you want anything.' At the door he turned and looked back at her, his eyes warm. 'Oh, and Miss Lennox——'

'Yes?'

'Good luck with the thinking,' he said softly; and was gone.

Julia did not move. She felt winded, as if she had been hurt mortally but so shocked by the blow that she had not yet begun to experience the pain.

A child! How could she not have known? Why had she never considered the possibility? Yet during all those hours of passion and their anguished aftermath she had never even thought of such a thing.

'I'm so *stupid*!' she said aloud, furiously.

She put her hand under her heart and winced. The cracked rib made itself felt, but she was almost glad of it. A cracked rib was a little thing to bear compared with the enormity of a lost baby. She shut her eyes, screwing them up tight against the pain. It was like the end of the world. She had had a chance to have Roberto's child, to carry it

and love it and make a home for it, and now, because of
her own stupidity and recklessness, that chance was
gone. She felt a great rush of despair engulf her. The
chance would not come again, she knew.

Julia lay for a long while, letting the tears seep out of
her, not loudly but with infinite pain. When the nurse
came in two hours later she looked at her with concern.

'Do you want anything, Miss Lennox?'

Julia managed a smile. 'No, thank you.'

It was not true. She wanted her baby back. She wanted
that chance. Most of all she wanted Roberto. She wanted
his strength and his laughter and his arms round her and,
above all, she wanted the prospect that he would be here
tomorrow and the day after, for the rest of her life.

'Are you sure?'

'Quite sure. I've got all I need,' said Julia desolately.

And that was true. She would survive, even without
her child, even without Roberto's love. She was a
survivor and she would not collapse. But there were
degrees of need, and she knew that without Roberto's
passion and companionship, she would be damaged
irreparably. She faced the thought squarely, just as she
faced the thought that she would not see him again. If she
had had his child he might, perhaps, have come to her at
least occasionally. And if not, she would have had the
baby to love. Without it, she had no call on him and her
life would be a desert.

She said none of this to the nurse, to the doctors who
came to see her later or even to Tony Gallasay, her long-
time friend and partner in Technica. It hurt desperately,
but it was private. To talk of it seemed almost like a
betrayal of Roberto and everything she felt for him.

It was Tony who came to take her back to New York.
He breezed into her hospital bedroom with a sheaf of
flowers like a bridal bouquet and a grin like the Cheshire

Cat.

'Hi there, my lovely. This is a great day,' he said, swooping her up in a bearhug. 'Technica ceases to totter.'

Julia returned his embrace gratefully. 'Have you missed me?'

'You wait till you see your in-box—that will show you how we've missed you!' He picked up her small overnight bag. 'Is this everything?'

She nodded. 'All my luggage was left behind in Alto Rio. I'm even light one passport.'

'Good,' he said, tucking his other arm round her and leading her out of the door. 'That will mean that you won't go winging off to a Caribbean island before I've had time to sob all my problems out on your shoulder.'

'Problems?' Julia asked warily, knowing Tony for a great but impressionable philanderer. 'You're not in love again?'

He looked injured. 'What do you mean, again? I've been in love faithfully with the same woman for,' he thought about it, 'two whole months.'

'Then it's a new lady since I last saw you,' Julia pointed out tranquilly.

They were going out through the automatic doors into the sunshine, and for a moment she flinched. It was too reminiscent of the village, that brilliant light. Then she steadied herself. Tony was still talking. He had not noticed.

'It's all very well, you woman with a heart of stone,' he complained. 'I can't help it if I've got an affectionate temperament. It can be hellish uncomfortable—you don't know!'

Don't I? thought Julia, saying nothing. He helped her into the car. She noted from the logo on the side that it belonged to one of Technica's Florida customers. Tony must have borrowed it for the occasion. It was very luxurious with a privacy panel between the passengers and the uniformed driver.

When he had got in beside her, Tony said in a sober voice, 'Honey, I want to tell you that I know about the baby. The doctors told me—I guess they must have thought I was your husband or something. I'm sorry.'

Julia flinched, and he took her hand comfortingly.

'I know it's a silly thing to say right now, but try to forget it. It wasn't your fault and you're not to blame yourself.' His voice roughened. 'And if I ever get my hands on the bastard that did it to you, I'll make him regret the day he was born!'

'Please, I—don't want to talk about it,' she begged.

'No, I guess not.' But he was too kind, he cared for her too much, he would not be deflected from his purpose of comforting her. 'Julia, rape is just another sort of violence. You're no more to blame than if you'd been mugged. You were injured and it's over. Now you have to put it behind you and get on with your life.'

Julia gave a broken laugh that was half a sob. 'I know,' she said. 'But *please*, Tony, no more.'

'OK, no more for now. But promise me you'll come to me if you feel bad about it. Talking helps.'

'So I'm told,' she said, trying to smile.

'And,' he added with a return to cheerfulness, 'you've got far too much work waiting for you to consider a nervous breakdown until well into next year!'

She squeezed his fingers, then, 'Thank you,' she said with real gratitude.

He was as good as his word. Julia was able, without any spinning out of work, to spend ten hours a day at her desk in her office and another two or three when she got home to her Manhattan apartment. It got her through the first frightful weeks when, at every post, she looked for a letter from Roberto; when every time the telephone rang she felt sick and had to force herself to pick it up. She never worked out whether she was most afraid that it would be Roberto or that it would not. It never was. The desolation hit her every time and did not lessen.

She told herself that she had not expected anything else. Sometimes he had looked at her as if he hated her; on several occasions he had more or less said that he did. There was no reason for him to seek her out. He must be glad that he had got her out of his hair at such a convenient time and with no little effort on his part.

The revolution in Oaxacan was over. The papers reported approvingly that it had been peacefully accomplished and that the former President had been allowed to retire to his country estate, retaining all his military honours which he had won when he was General in Chief of the country's army. It was a copybook change of government, no victimisation, no bloodshed, no mass flight of the supporters of the former régime.

The new President was much praised. Julia read about him, hoping for a sight of Roberto's name, but there was none. The new President was called Quintano. He came from an old family, and his grandfather had been President in the forties. He was widely travelled and much respected internationally. He had surrounded himself with a team of intelligent patriots of mixed political views. After weeks of reading the papers avidly, Julia had to concede that Roberto was not among them.

It was then that the new, corrosive, fear began. Was he hurt? The revolution might be said to be bloodless, but that could be journalists' exaggeration. They could mean relatively bloodless. Roberto could be an insignificant statistic, not worth reporting, and still be dead.

In the end she could bear it no longer and she telephoned Larry, who was still conducting negotiations with the Oaxacatecan Government, but he was virtually no use at all. He had never met Roberto, did not remember him and had never heard the name mentioned. But he could tell her that there had been no casualties in the new government takeover. And if a prominent lawyer had had an accident the little newspapers of Alto Rio would have been full of it. He promised to make enquiries when he went back but suggested, with profound indifference, that the guy had probably gone back to making money now that the coup was over. And if he was an international lawyer, that probably meant he was travelling.

Julia agreed and thanked him. After that, of course, she was braced for a ring on the doorbell as well as a letter or phone call. They never came.

CHAPTER TEN

IN the end it was Larry who, inadvertently, put an end to it all. He called Julia at home late one night. She was wearily picking her way through a column of figures for the third time, wondering why they did not balance, and almost did not pick up the telephone. After the twentieth ring, though, she succumbed to curiosity.

'Julia?' asked Larry. 'Did I get you out of the bath?'

'No,' she said, thinking wryly that her desk, though awash with papers, did not really qualify for that description. 'What can I do for you, Larry?'

'Well, it's a bit awkward,' he said, gearing himself up to ask what was clearly a favour. 'And Tony said I wasn't to.'

'Oh?' She was intrigued.

'It's the Cascadas project. We've got a signing ceremony at the Goldcrest Hotel—big party, television cameras, the whole works. The President is flying in for it.'

'So?' Julia was noticeably cooler.

'Well, you see Julia, I keep getting these messages that they want you there.'

She went cold. 'Why?' she asked at last.

She could almost see him shrug at the other end of the line. 'Who knows? I gave up trying to understand clients years ago. What they want, they want, and there's an end of it. I guess they want to build bridges or something—because you were kidnapped and all.'

'I see,' she said slowly. So it was not some ploy of Roberto's. That was a relief but it was also a disappointment.

'Tony said you'd taken all you were going to take from the bastards and I wasn't to mention the thing to you, but I get the idea the other side really think it's important.'

'Perhaps they want public forgiveness,' said Julia wryly.

'You can see their point. They're a new government and they keep telling the world how civilised they are. They can't afford to have former kidnap victims ready to tell the press about them,' said Larry with surprising shrewdness.

'Maybe they'll offer me a pension,' said Julia with irony. 'All right, I take your point. When is this jamboree?'

He told her the date, and she looked in her diary. She had to go to Washington that week, but she could switch days easily enough if she wanted to. Did she want to?

She said slowly, 'It may be all right. I'll try, Larry. Is there,' she cleared her throat, 'is there any chance of me seeing a guest list?'

'Sure.' Even on such half-hearted agreement, Larry was elated. 'I'll let your secretary have a copy tomorrow first thing. You're a great girl, Julia. It's a privilege to work with you!'

She realised the reason for his exuberant gratitude when she looked at the guest list the next morning. President, Finance Minister, Economy Minister, Central Bank Governor, Secretary of the State Mining Corporation, they were all there. No wonder Larry was willing to defy Tony in order to keep them happy!

Julia ran her eye carefully down the list. Roberto's name was mentioned nowhere, though there was a Señor M. Olivados from the Planning Ministry who might, she supposed, turn out to be Miguel. That gave her pause. Did she want to meet Miguel? Could she face meeting him? And what if he tried to talk to her about Roberto?

She picked up her telephone, reaching a sudden compromise.

'I'll come, Larry,' she told him crisply. 'But I have to get to Washington, so I'll need to leave early. If you explain, I'm sure your guests won't be offended.'

'Great!' he said. 'I'll see Mary Lou has a car waiting to take you to the airport.'

'I rely on you then,' said Julia and added teasingly, 'And make sure it comes off your budget and not mine!'

The signing ceremony was at three. In the end, Julia did not make it because she was engaged in a vital transcontinental telephone call and Larry's secretary, after hovering in the door of her office for ten minutes, had eventually shrugged and gone away. So Julia went later, on her own, well after the official party. She arrived at the hotel in time to catch only the last speech, by the Mining Minister, before the reception dissolved into the usual party-like atmosphere.

She could not see Larry anywhere. She caught sight of several journalists she knew, and one of them, a woman with a nose for the personal angle even in commercial stories, was clearly curious.

'You have no hard feelings?'

'Hard feelings?' Julia echoed, smiling. She sipped her drink. 'Why should I? They've just signed a multi-million-dollar contract with my company.'

'Over the kidnap.'

Julia shrugged. 'One of the hazards of my profession. I don't suppose race-track drivers have hard feelings towards the cars they drive, either, and they're pretty dangerous too.'

'So you weren't badly treated?' The woman's eyes were avid.

Julia gave her a sweet smile. 'I had simple food, fresh

air and plenty of exercise—to say nothing of being away
from my desk. People pay large sums of money to have
rest cures like that.'

'Weren't you frightened? Not at all?'

Julia looked round the room for someone to help her
escape this inquisition.

'I'm not a fool. I'm afraid of a lot of things, including
the New York subway,' she said drily.

'Of course, you're British, aren't you?' the woman
remarked, though Julia did not know whether she
attributed to that the fact that Julia was afraid of the
subway or was equally afraid of other things.

'Scottish,' she corrected. 'But I've been here a long
time, so I've acclimatised. And I'm still scared of the
subway.'

'And not scared of your kidnappers?' asked her
interrogator shrewdly. 'There were rumours, I remember. Do you share their beliefs, Miss Lennox? Or are you
perhaps romantically involved with one of them?'

Julia froze her with a look. 'I'm an agronomist,' she
said coolly. 'My only romantic attachment is to insectici-
de,' and she looked meaningly at the woman who
flushed. 'Excuse me, I see someone over there I must
speak to,' she added, lying courteously.

Julia walked away. She was shaken, furious and
something else. She felt faintly apprehensive, as if she
were under attack from an unknown quarter. She sipped
her drink, scanning the room, and suddenly, startlingly,
came face to face with Miguel Olivados.

But this was a different Miguel. In a smart suit and
expensive tie, he looked efficient and unapproachable.
He also seemed less than pleased to see her.

'So you came,' he greeted her abruptly. 'I wondered
whether you would.'

Julia made a face. 'I was told to.'

'So I imagined.'

She was chilled by his manner. 'How are you, Miguel? And the others?'

He gave her a look of dislike. 'Do you care?'

She gasped. 'Of course I care! You were very good to me.'

'But you ran away from us, the first chance you got,' he said.

Julia stared at him. 'What do you mean?'

'When Augusto brought that lorry back. You just jumped in it and took off—without a backward look, though Roberto was fighting for his life.'

As she whitened he said more gently, 'You cannot deny this, Julia. I saw it with my own eyes.'

Her eyes were dark pools of horror. 'Was he—hurt?'

Miguel's own eyes narrowed. 'By Augusto? No.'

She said almost to herself, 'I didn't realise. All I could think of was that Augusto had betrayed him, that I had to get the radio truck away from the village . . .'

Miguel looked thunderstruck. 'Is this the truth?'

Julia did not reply, but her evident misery answered for her.

Miguel said in a more moderate tone, 'You did not know that Augusto had pulled a knife on Roberto?'

Her hands flew to her cheeks. 'No!' It was a little animal cry of distress.

'Hush, hush—I have said, he was not hurt.' Miguel sounded positively soothing. He looked round the room, at the chattering oblivious throng, and his mouth tightened. 'I suppose you have not talked to him?'

'To Roberto?' Julia shook her head.

'And he, of course, would not force himself on you after you ran away from him.' She began to protest, but Miguel raised a pacifying hand. 'As he thought. As he still thinks.' He was thoughtful. 'This puts a new complexion on things.'

'Does it?' said Julia, uncomprehending and very unhappy.

'Yes, I——' But they were interrupted.

'Ah, Miss Lennox, you're here.' It was Tony, hugely formal but with a definite smile in his eyes for her. 'Mr President, may I introduce Miss Julia Lennox, our agronomist director. Miss Lennox, President Quintano.'

'Oh, God!' murmured Miguel under his breath. Julia heard him distinctly. She was not surprised.

Because the exquisitely groomed and perfectly mannered President was Roberto Madariaga. In a daze she put out a hand. He kissed it, coldly, making the gesture a mockery. Something inside Julia iced over, hard, at that scornful kiss.

'Miss Lennox, it is a delight to meet you again,' he said smoothly.

She must get away. She must get away *now*.

She made an effort at a civil smile, but she was clearly less successful than Roberto, and Tony looked at her speculatively.

'Mr President,' she murmured, freeing her hand from his.

Miguel spoke to Roberto across their heads, holding his eyes meaningly. 'I had not realised how much we owe Miss Lennox,' he said with great deliberation.

Roberto smiled, a meaningless stretching of the firm mouth that had kissed her, that she had kissed. Julia felt faint with the sharpness of too explicit memories. Oh God, she had to get away before she broke down and reached for him!

'I am properly impressed by her presence here this afternoon,' he told Miguel, and then to Julia, 'A charitable gesture, Miss Lennox. It cannot be pleasant for you to be reminded of that unhappy time.'

A little gust of anger shook Julia. How dared he stand there and look so remote and bait her as if it was she, and not he, who was indifferent?

'It's not,' she agreed, politely. 'But it's in the past and must be forgotten.'

'Indubitably. How very philosophical of you!' He was suave, but the tone bit like acid.

She shifted, looked at her watch, addressed herself to Tony.

'I'm afraid I shall have to be going—my flight is in half an hour.'

'Miss Lennox is going to Washington,' Tony explained. 'She had to postpone a meeting in order to be here.'

'I am even more impressed,' drawled Roberto.

'Good. That was the object of the exercise,' Julia told him, hating him and giving him a brilliant smile. 'But now . . .'

'There is no need for you to leave us, Miss Lennox. I am myself going to Washington after the reception. You may join me on the Presidential plane.' He sounded amused. 'So you can avoid the hustle of the commercial flight and we will be able to discuss old times.'

Julia was appalled. 'That's very kind of you, but . . .'

Tony, for some reason best known to himself said, 'Yes, why don't you, Julia? You know you haven't got any important meetings until tomorrow and you'll arrive in plenty of time for dinner with Steve.'

Roberto's eyes narrowed. 'Steve?' he enquired haughtily.

'The Chairman of a firm that does a lot of work with us,' explained Tony blithely. 'He always gives us dinner when one of us flies in.'

'I see.' Roberto's smile at Julia was blatant mockery. 'So it seems to be settled, Miss Lennox. Be ready to leave in forty minutes, if you please.'

He gave her a nod and strolled away, Tony in attendance.

'Phew!' said Miguel on a long whistle. 'He is not in a nice mood!'

Julia felt transfixed with pain. Her face felt stiff and her mouth was dry as the dust of that unforgotten mountainside.

'Why is he doing this?' she said wretchedly.

Miguel sighed. 'At a guess, I'd say it was because he's as angry as I've ever seen him. He was—not pleased when you ran away.'

Julia shut her eyes. 'I wish I'd never met him!' she said fervently.

Miguel did not answer directly. 'I had better make sure his aides know the arrangements,' he said, sighing, 'otherwise we are quite likely to take off leaving you stranded until the next shuttle leaves.'

She nodded and he left her. She wondered for a hectic minute or two whether anyone would notice if she slipped away and took the Washington shuttle anyway. But almost at once she rejected the idea. It would be an open insult to a visiting head of state—and quite unforgivable to anyone who did not know what had passed between herself and Roberto. Somehow she would just have to gather her courage into both hands and make conversation with his entourage until they touched down in Washington and she could make her escape. After that, she promised herself, she was never going to put herself in a twenty-mile radius of the man ever again.

But there was no entourage to talk to, as she found with dismay once on board. She had been taken to the airport by the car arranged by Larry. The President, it was explained to her, would run the gamut of reporters and photographers and then travel separately. It was not explained to her that he would also be travelling alone.

She was seated in one of the royal blue velvet seats with the national arms embroidered on the head-rest when he arrived. The steward, discreet and efficient, served them with a bottle of wine and two glasses and retired into the crew's quarters, after closing and bolting the air-locked door. Julia watched this manoeuvre with horror.

'Are we . . . That is, are you . . .'

'We are alone,' Roberto confirmed, amused. 'Apart from the crew, of course, who will not intrude. I gather it will be some time before we get clearance to take off. Have a drink.'

'No, thank you.'

He shrugged. 'As you wish.' He poured himself some of the blood-dark wine and held it to his lips, watching her over it. 'Do you dislike wine?'

'I don't drink when I'm travelling,' said Julia, who hated flying and had been sick on more than one occasion on a turbulent flight.

'How wise,' he murmured. 'What a paragon of all the virtues you are!'

She looked at him with manifest dislike. 'Do you have this aeroplane all to yourself?' she enquired, changing the subject with determination.

'You sound as if you disapprove of my humble Presidential perk,' he mocked.

She shrugged. 'I wouldn't have thought your country could afford it, that's all.'

If her object was to anger him she did not succeed. His look of amusement deepened.

'And you are, of course, right. This machine belongs to the civil airline. They have lent it to us for this trip. I am going on to Europe later, you know.'

'No, I didn't.' She was genuinely interested, but it was also a safe subject. 'Is this part of your bridge-mending policy?'

'Absolutely.' He poured more wine and settled back in his seat, describing his government's strategy.

Julia listened with interest as she watched him. He was thinner, and he had lost that devastatingly attractive tan. His skin had a faint grey tinge to it now, and his eyes were shadowed as if he spent too long scanning documents in artificial light. When he tipped his head back and closed his eyes, the arrogant profile was etched bleakly. She wondered, suddenly, whether being President had put him under the kind of strain he could not handle. She would have thought he could master anything, but she sensed an oblique tension in him which made her wonder whether she was wrong.

He was silent during take-off. When they were airborne he addressed a couple of remarks to her but his mind was clearly elsewhere. At length he asked whether she would object if he read some of his briefing material, and she was grateful. She fell silent, trying to ignore the fact that, sitting next to him with his shoulder touching hers and his expression completely indifferent, her nerves were stretched to shattering tension.

Probably it was because of this that she felt a slight queasiness, for the flight could not have been smoother. With a murmured apology she excused herself and went to the tiny washroom compartment. It had been fitted out for the flight with monogrammed handtowels and brushes and combs bearing the national coat of arms. She smiled wryly, rinsing her face and running her wrists under cold water. Perhaps she ought to purloin one of the blue-bordered towels as a souvenir.

Roberto looked up when she made her way back down the plane.

'You are better?'

Julia was startled and showed it. She had not said she was feeling unwell. His mouth compressed.

'It was evident,' he said with something of a snap, answering her unspoken question. His steep lids drooped. 'You have suffered ill-effects from the abortion?' he asked coolly.

Julia felt as if the plane had dropped ten thousand feet. She sat down hard in an aisle seat and stared at him.

His mouth twisted. 'Now you are going to ask me how I knew that,' he observed. 'And, like the other, it is evident. When you—left us—you were pregnant. Now you are not. And you spent ten days in what I believe is a very exclusive Florida clinic.'

'You're very well informed,' Julia said at last, thinly.

'Naturally.' Roberto sounded indifferent to the point of boredom. 'It was, after all, my child.'

Suddenly, inexplicably, tears filled her eyes, and she turned her head away.

'Yes,' she said in a muffled voice, 'it was.'

'It did not occur to you that I might have been consulted?' He sounded like a lawyer, she thought, logical and unmoved. And accusing. 'Or even concerned?'

'I—No. No it didn't.' Her voice was shaky. 'You never tried to contact me. I didn't think you would care.'

'Not care about my child?' Not so unmoved, after all, but not moved by Julia.

She straightened. 'I didn't realise that you knew about the child.'

She looked up and met a gaze full of irony. 'My good girl, we were living as closely as two people can and you were exhibiting all the signs. Even though you chose not to tell me, how could I not know?'

She thought, painfully, ruefully, how she had not

known. Her expression was wry.

'Why do you look like that?' There was feeling licking through his voice now—anger? 'Do you think I was so little aware of you that I could ignore such things?'

Julia shook her head, the dark hair swinging. 'I never thought about it at all.'

There was a long silence, then Roberto said bleakly, 'I see.'

Julia studied the backs of her hands as if the secrets of the world were lined on them.

Eventually he said with what appeared to be an effort. 'Miguel tells me I owe you an apology.'

'I'm sure you don't,' she murmured, confused.

'For misinterpreting your actions that last day as a bolt for freedom,' he went on, ignoring her. 'I am told that you were trying to remove incriminating evidence from the village.'

'Yes,' she said, not looking at him.

'That was very brave of you.' He sounded stiff.

She shrugged. 'Not really. If it stayed there I should have been flattened along with the village—Augusto made it very plain that that was the idea. If I got it far enough away, the village escaped and so, perhaps might I.' She smiled, a little blindly. 'As I did.'

Roberto muttered, 'Oh God!' under his breath.

'What?' She did not understand.

'Do you realise how nearly you *didn't* escape?' Suddenly his voice was rough, tortured. 'Don't you know that if that bloody truck had tilted the other way, you would still have been in it and would almost certainly have been killed?'

'Would I?' Julia was surprised. She had never thought very much about that last ride. In retrospect it seemed shifting, like a picture seen through moving water. She was not sure how much of what she remembered of it was real and how much she had dreamed. She shook her head. 'It all seems so far away now.'

'Does it?' Roberto was grim. He swung round on her and seized her hands, and startled, she glanced up. The look of strain was pronounced. 'It doesn't to me. It's a nightmare I carry with me constantly—you hurt and me helpless and the whole damned world going up in flames!'

She stared at him, and he gave an impatient sigh.

'I promised myself I wouldn't inflict this on you. I swore I wouldn't. But ever since Miguel told me, I've been wondering and calculating and hoping till I can't think straight.' He gave her hands a little shake. 'Julia, will you answer me one question, and answer it truthfully?'

She could not have withstood the pleading note in the low voice even if she wanted to.

'Yes,' she said simply.

As if he could not help himself Roberto put out a hand and tucked one soft strand of dark hair very gently behind her ear.

'Could you ever forgive me?'

There was a long silence. Whatever Julia had expected it was not that. She was nonplussed and had no answer.

Roberto said huskily, 'I know—I knew at the time— that I wasn't fair to you. I just took what I wanted. I have no excuse but that—then it all seemed so precarious. We might never have had another chance. And I was terrified that everything would end and we would never have taken our chance. Can you understand that?'

Julia nodded slowly.

'God knows, I never meant to hurt you.' He leaned forward urgently. 'Do you believe that?'

She said wonderingly, 'But you seemed so angry—all the time.'

He groaned. 'So I was, but not with you.'

'What, then?'

'Oh, the times, the whole stupid situation. And you being in danger—that was insupportable.'

Seeing the expression of naked pain on his face, Julia believed him. She drew a deep breath. He had spoken of chances and this was one, now, that she had to take, although she knew she risked rejection, humiliation and worse sorrow than she had faced so far when she did not, quite, know the answer.

She took a deep breath and asked very steadily, 'Did you ever love me?'

His hands tightened on hers until she could have cried out.

'What are you saying?' Roberto's voice was hoarse.

But she could not repeat it. Once had cost her too much. Her eyes fell before his, her lashes fluttering against her hot cheeks.

'But surely—how could you not know? God in Heaven,' he groaned despairingly, 'every shepherd boy for miles knew that Madariaga had lost his head completely over the foreign lady with sky-blue eyes!'

Julia was so startled she jumped, her eyes flying to his. He smiled at her very tenderly.

'Did you not know that was what they called you?' He touched one finger to the corner of her eye. 'Quite rightly. That was the first thing I noticed about you—eyes the colour of the morning sky. I was horrified when I found that they belonged to Pepe's prize prisoner!'

She said, 'That was the first time you were angry with me.'

'Angry,' said Roberto, reflectively. 'That is a little mild for what I felt. You sat there, so beautiful in that silly evening dress, so groggy that I was not sure that you were even focusing properly, and so brave. And that child

Pepe was already making indecent suggestions. I could have torn the place apart, I was so furious. And instead I had to be judicious and calm and polite!'

Julia's hands turned in his, returning his clasp.

'So you weren't as hostile as you seemed? Sometimes I thought you hated me, I was so in the way.'

'Hated you!' He sounded horrified. 'How can you say that? It must have been obvious at least that I wanted you; right from the start.'

'They can go together,' pointed out Julia drily.

'Can they?' Roberto shook his head. 'I can't imagine it. Certainly never with you. All I wanted, ever, was to get you out of there and keep you safe and hope that, in time, you might come to love me too.'

'In time?'

He sighed. 'Yes, I know—we didn't *have* any time. That's why I forced the pace like that. And all the time I could feel you slipping further and further away from me. To begin with you were attracted, I knew that, but then, after I had made love to you, you grew so remote. You could talk all day to Angelina or to Olivados, but at night, with me, nothing. You were so gentle and it seemed as if all I was doing was hurting you. And then, when Angelina told me that you were expecting my child——'

He stood up suddenly and walked to a porthole, keeping his back to her.

'I waited and waited for you to tell me,' he said in a low voice. 'Once you virtually admitted it, when I asked whether you had talked to Miguel. But you never did.'

'Why should I have told Miguel?' asked Julia, puzzled.

'He is a doctor,' Roberto reminded her.

'I'd forgotten.'

'It was then that I realised I had been fooling myself, that you really did detest and despise me, when you would not even tell me about our child. When you ran away, it just seemed to confirm my worst fears.'

Julia stood up and went to him, sliding her hand into his.

'Roberto, you will despise me when I tell you this. I did not know about the child.'

He looked down at her from his great height, his eyes very dark and questioning.

'Truly. Angelina may have known the signs. I didn't. The first I knew about it was when the doctor told me I had lost it' She looked down at their clasped hands. 'I— was devastated. If I'd known I would have wanted it so much.' Her voice sank to a whisper. 'I wanted you so much then. I was lonely for you every night.'

Roberto said as if he did not dare to believe it, 'But you said nothing. All those hours when we made love, nothing. Not even my name. When I loved you so much . . .'

He dragged her into his arms and kissed her almost savagely, and Julia responded eagerly, half sobbing, her hands holding his head as they had done so many times before.

He said at last, his breathing ragged, 'Will you marry me?'

'Whenever you want.'

He held her away from him, as if he could not quite believe it.

'You mean that,' he said at last, slowly.

She nodded, eyes shining.

'You'll forgive me? Forget the way I hurt you, insulted you, bullied you . . .'

'If you'll do the same for me. I don't recall that I took it all tamely,' said Julia. 'I can remember trading insults in my turn.'

At last a touch of that old amusement returned. 'Oh, you did! I'd never paid court to a more argumentative lady. You ignored me, contradicted me and made it plain that you did not care whether you saw me or not.' He hugged her against him. 'If it hadn't been for the way you made love to me, I would have given up long ago!'

Julia blushed but said soberly, 'I'm glad about that. I thought I was just a temporary diversion. For the duration of the revolution only.'

His lips moved in her hair. 'How can you have been that stupid?' Roberto murmured lovingly.

'Well, you never spoke of *feelings*,' she pointed out with justified indignation, 'only attraction and wanting. And then, do you remember, when you said what had I got to make a fuss about, I wasn't a virgin, was I? You sounded so contemptuous.'

'You're a fool,' he informed her. 'What have I got to be contemptuous about? I was not a virgin either. And I don't believe in the double standard.'

'Then why did you ask?' Julia was bewildered. That little memory had stung for a long time.

'Because I wanted to know.' said Roberto, exasperated. 'It would have made a difference, surely you can see that?'

'Would it?' She looked at him doubtfully. 'You mean you wouldn't have taken me to bed?'

Roberto was shaken by a little laugh. 'No, I don't think I can lay claim to quite such scrupulousness as that! But I would not have pushed the relationship so fast. Which would,' he added reflectively, 'have been better, I suspect. That virginal air of yours was not entirely misleading.'

'What do you mean?'

He looked down at her gravely. 'You were much more inexperienced than I had expected, more vulnerable, more unsure of yourself—and so, more unsure of me. I did not realise so I did not deal with it properly.' His eyes darkened. 'You should never have had to ask whether I loved you.'

'And now that I have?'

Roberto held her against him, his hand moulding her shoulder, not entirely steadily.

'You know. I have never loved anyone as I love you. I did not realise I was capable of it.' He was wry. 'Oh, I liked women, enjoyed their company, and had great fun going to bed with one or two. But nothing like this. I never felt as if I'd found the other side of myself before. If you won't marry me, then I shall never marry,' he said simply. 'There could not be anyone else.'

Julia gave a long sigh. 'That's a relief,' she said drily, but her eyes were warm. 'Though is it going to be good for you to marry a foreigner? As you're President, I mean.'

'I shan't always be President,' said Roberto, amused. 'And my staff will be offering up prayers that I can persuade you to marry me. Believe me.'

She pulled a little away from him. 'Your *staff*? What do they know about it?'

His eyes danced. 'Apart from Miguel, not very much. But they must guess quite a lot. From my evil temper, for one thing—I have always been the most patient of men up to now. And from the way I have seized every letter and telex from Technica over the last months.' His mouth quirked. 'And the fact that I turned them all off this plane must have given them something of a clue, wouldn't you think?'

Understanding began to dawn. 'You turned them off this plane so we could be alone?' gasped Julia, impressed and amused at the same time.

'Absolutely.'

'But—what have you done with them? Where are they?'

He chuckled. 'Queueing for the Washington shuttle, I imagine.'

'Roberto, that's shocking!' Julia told him, trying and failing not to laugh. 'They could be waiting all night!'

He looked solemn 'That was also in their instructions.'

'Oh.'

She felt the familiar wave of shivery desire start to flicker deep inside her, and she moistened her lips. She was not nervous, of course she was not, she loved him and trusted him and was secure in the knowledge that he loved her. Nevertheless, she could not meet his eyes.

'You know, it's silly, but I think I feel shy,' she said conversationally.

Roberto took her comprehensively into his arms.

His voice was low. 'Please stay with me tonight. We'll get married as soon as you like in Washington or London or Paris or Alto Rio, I don't care. But don't leave me again,' he said unevenly. 'Not yet. Not until I've convinced myself this is real .'

Julia gave a long sigh, resting her head against his chest.

'I feel like that too. But won't it be embarrassing?'

His eyes glinted down at her. 'You are ashamed of loving me?'

Julia kissed him. 'No, of course not.'

'You are ashamed of having me love you, perhaps?' His hands moved beautifully down her body until she trembled.

She gave a shaky laugh. 'Not ashamed. A bit uncertain maybe.' A thought occurred to her. 'Hell, I don't even know your name. Tony said you were President Quintano.'

His lips were travelling softly over her face. 'That is a fancy of my staff,' he said dismissively. 'My maternal grandfather was President before me. As you know,

Spanish surnames have both the father's and the mother's name included, though generally we only use the father's. But for a touch of instant tradition, they thought it would be a good idea if I used my mother's. It is sensible and will make it easier to slip back into my legal practice under my ordinary name when my term of office is over. Satisfied?'

'Relieved,' she corrected. She moved her body against him, laughing softly. 'I believe I shall have to wait for satisfaction.'

He caught his breath, but when he spoke his voice was full of affectionate amusement. 'Serves you right! you have made me wait for months. I shall see that you make it up to me.'

And later, in the Presidential suite at which all his staff had tactfully failed to arrive that night, he did. Freed from the constraints of uncertainty and fear, Julia responded with the absolute love she had always partially suppressed before. Afterwards they were both silent, shaken to the depths by their feelings and their power over each other. They lay, hands loosely clasped, in peaceful companionship.

Roberto said, 'You must never mistrust me again.'

'No,' she agreed quietly.

He kissed her shoulder. 'If you are uncertain, you must tell me.'

'I'm not,' said Julia. She moved, stretching languorously. A hint of mischief came into her voice. 'How could I be?'

He kissed her again. 'But seriously, we must talk more. For instance, your career is important to you, I know. You must not give it up. We can arrange things. It will be easier, of course, when I am no longer President. Perhaps,' he said reflectively, 'it would be a good idea to have the children now, so that you can return to your career full time after my term of office is over. What do you think?'

She stroked one finger very delicately along his lips. 'I think I'd rather wait and see. I'm not feeling like long range planning at the moment.'

Roberto bit her finger. 'I am just trying to communicate,' he said in an injured voice.

She laughed. 'There are other ways.'

'Fine, fine,' he grumbled. 'There I am trying to be a supportive and liberated husband and all you can think of is sex.'

'Yup.' She moved sinuously against him.

'Maybe you're right,' he agreed. When his lips met hers, she could feel he was laughing. 'I can't concentrate on conversation when you feel like this against me anyway.' The slow fires began to burn as they moved, touched, entwined. 'I suppose the only communication I really need is for you to tell me you love me, *mi amor*,' he said huskily.

Julia did. Not just in words.

Harlequin Presents

Coming Next Month

983 STANDING ON THE OUTSIDE Lindsay Armstrong
An Australian secretary is drawn out when her new boss goes out of his way to make her smile…enjoy life again. But what's the point if his heart still belongs to his childhood sweetheart?

984 DON'T ASK ME NOW Emma Darcy
How can a country girl from Armidale trust her heart to her uppercrust business partner? Especially when his attraction coincides with the renewed interest of the first man to reject her as not being good enough to marry.

985 ALL MY TOMORROWS Rosemary Hammond
In war-torn San Cristobal a nurse falls hard for an injured reporter, who then disappears from her life. She knows she must forget him. But how can she, when he finds her again in her home town.

986 FASCINATION Patricia Lake
Emotionally scarred by the last suitor shoved her way, a young American finds a merchant banker difficult to trust—particularly when their bedside wedding in her grandfather's hospital room is arranged by her grandfather and the groom!

987 LOVE IN THE DARK Charlotte Lamb
The barrister an Englishwoman once loved threatens to revive the scandal that drove them apart five years ago—unless she breaks off with her fiancé and marries him instead.

988 A GAME OF DECEIT Sandra Marton
A magazine reporter, traveling incognito, wangles an invitation to stay at a famous actor's private hideaway in the Mexican Sierra Madre. But she's the one who begins to feel vulnerable, afraid of being exposed.

989 VELVET PROMISE Carole Mortimer
A young divorcée returns to Jersey and falls in love with her ex-husband's cousin. But he still thinks she married for money. If only she could tell him how horribly wrong he is!

990 BITTERSWEET MARRIAGE Jeneth Murrey
Turndowns confuse a job-hunting woman until she discovers the souce of her bad luck—the powerful English businessman she once walked out on. Finally he's in a position to marry her!

Available in June wherever paperback books are sold, or through Harlequin Reader Service:

In the U.S.
901 Fuhrmann Blvd.
P.O. Box 1397
Buffalo, N.Y. 14240-1397

In Canada
P.O. Box 603
Fort Erie, Ontario
L2A 5X3

Take 4 books & a surprise gift FREE

SPECIAL LIMITED-TIME OFFER

Mail to   **Harlequin Reader Service**®

In the U.S.   In Canada
901 Fuhrmann Blvd.   P.O. Box 609
P.O. Box 1394   Fort Erie, Ontario
Buffalo, N.Y. 14240-1394   L2A 5X3

YES!   Please send me 4 free Harlequin Romance® novels
and my free surprise gift. Then send me 6 brand-new novels every
month as they come off the presses. Bill me at the low price of
$1.66 each*—a 15% saving off the retail price. There are no
shipping, handling or other hidden costs. There is no minimum
number of books I must purchase. I can always return a shipment
and cancel at any time. Even if I never buy another book from
Harlequin, the 4 free novels and the surprise gift are mine to keep
forever.   116 BPR BP7S

*$1.75 in Canada plus 69¢ postage and handling per shipment.

Name _____ (PLEASE PRINT)

Address _____ Apt. No. _____

City _____ State/Prov. _____ Zip/Postal Code _____

This offer is limited to one order per household and not valid to present
subscribers. Price is subject to change.   DOR-SUB-1A

ATTRACTIVE, SPACE SAVING BOOK RACK

Display your most prized novels on this handsome and sturdy book rack. The hand-rubbed walnut finish will blend into your library decor with quiet elegance, providing a practical organizer for your favorite hard-or soft-covered books.

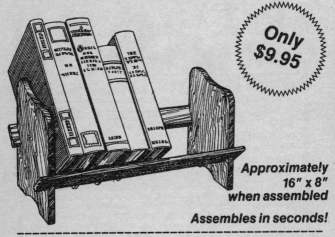

Only $9.95

Approximately 16" x 8" when assembled

Assembles in seconds!

To order, rush your name, address and zip code, along with a check or money order for $10.70* ($9.95 plus 75¢ postage and handling) payable to *Harlequin Reader Service*:

Harlequin Reader Service
Book Rack Offer
901 Fuhrmann Blvd.
P.O. Box 1325
Buffalo, NY 14269-1325

Offer not available in Canada.

*New York residents add appropriate sales tax.

BKR-1R

GILLIAN HALL

The magnificent novel of a woman fighting for her greatest passion— and for a love to fulfill her deepest desires.

Stages

The desire to break from an unbearable past takes prima ballerina Anna Duras to Broadway, in search of the happiness she once knew. The tumultuous changes that follow lead her to the triumph of new success . . . and the promise of her greatest love.

Available in MAY or reserve your copy for April shipping by sending your name, address, zip or postal code along with a check or money order for $4.70 (includes 75 cents for postage and handling) payable to Worldwide Library to:

In the U.S.	In Canada
Worldwide Library	Worldwide Library
901 Fuhrmann Blvd.	P.O. Box 609
Box 1325	Fort Erie, Ontario
Buffalo, NY 14269-1325	L2A 5X3

Please specify book title with your order.

🌐 **WORLDWIDE LIBRARY**

STA-1

**A novel of greed, corruption
and high-stakes power-playing
in the Manhattan real estate arena.**

CO-OP

DAVID WIND

As captivating as *Hotel*, as powerful as *Condominium*, CO-OP opens the door on the wheeling and dealing and manipulations, the passions and betrayals, involved in the conversion of a Manhattan apartment building into a glitzy co-op.

Available in JUNE or reserve your copy for May shipping by sending your name, address, zip or postal code along with a check or money order for $5.25 (includes 75 cents for postage and handling) payable to Worldwide Library to:

In the U.S.	In Canada
Worldwide Library	Worldwide Library
901 Fuhrmann Blvd.	P.O. Box 609
Box 1325	Fort Erie, Ontario
Buffalo, NY 14269-1325	L2A 5X3

Please specify book title with your order.

⊕ **WORLDWIDE LIBRARY**

COP-1